LIZ

by
Helen Wood

Order this book online at www.trafford.com
or email orders@trafford.com

Most Trafford titles are also available at major online book retailers.

Printed in the United States of America.

ISBN: 978-1-4269-6714-6 (sc)
ISBN: 978-1-4269-6903-4 (hc)
ISBN: 978-1-4269-6715-3 (e)

Library of Congress Control Number: 2011907481

Trafford rev. 05/10/2011

 www.trafford.com

North America & international
toll-free: 1 888 232 4444 (USA & Canada)
phone: 250 383 6864 ♦ fax: 812 355 4082

Chapter 1

The sun shone through the trees dappling the water beneath. She lay on a flat boulder enjoying this half an hour before turning her thoughts into actions. Liz had thought briefly how could she possibly stop the sale at this late stage but she dismissed it, her mind was made up.

She sprang up and jumped on to the riverbank turned and ran up the garden and let herself in at the side door. She had lifted the telephone and asked for Harry. Harry had been their solicitor ever since they had gone into the business of selling property. In level tones she had told him to withdraw the house indefinitely.

'Are you sure Liz?' Harry's voice had an element of surprise.

'Never as sure in my life.' she answered.

'Liz,' John Miller called as he breezed into the house. Liz emerged from the kitchen and looked at him squarely.

'Have you been in touch with Harry just now or vice versa?' she asked her husband.

'No, why has he been in contact with us?'

'No but I have, stopping the sale of the property.' said Liz calmly.

'You have done what!' said John.

'Taken the property off the market.'

Hearing this he went berserk.

'You cannot do that, you know perfectly well we have as good as sold it.'

Liz held her ground.

'Well I have spoken to Harry and he now knows the position.' She continued getting bolder by the minute.

'Another thing you never tell me anything these days. I want to know more about your deals. I have never really known the full facts of the property market and why are we selling this house?'

1

'Don't you realise the money from this house is spoken for, you stupid woman.' John butted in.

Disregarding his last remark she continued.

'Ever since I married you, true at first I liked the idea of moving around with you, selling one house, buying another, a bigger and better one than before but soon I wanted to put down roots, I wanted to settle in one place and get to know the people there and start living like them.'

John impatiently raised his arm.

'You never told me, why didn't you?'

Liz was furious. She could not contain herself.

'What do you mean? I really thought you too were in favour of it. It took me a long time to realise that it was the furthest thing from your mind.'

Even in those days power had gone to John's head and what Liz saw she did not like.

'But there is one thing I grant you.' Liz continued. 'You can get out of holes like no one else, so it won't be any problem getting out of this one.'

In the ten years they had been married, he had trailed Liz up and down the country often leaving her in hotel lounges while he made a killing on an unsuspecting family, getting a nice big wedge of the profit. He could hardly admit to himself that he had not taken time out to be with his wife. It was only dawning on him now that he should have heeded the warnings, small warnings then, but now the impact was rushing in on him.

From a distance Liz was saying something but for the minute he was seeing fleeting moments of the past when he should have taken Liz's advice instead of going on regardless. Only this morning he had been talking to a chap who had gone to the wall in the same business and now here was Liz stopping the sale of the house. How on earth was he going to intimate to her that it was imperative the sale should go through or they would end up in the bankruptcy court.

One could not say that John Miller was not clever in his business deals. He toured the countryside to acquire the right property in the right district for his clients. They in turn were up made with the quickness of the transaction and they would certainly put business his way, taking his card before parting and that was the case in many instances. Money was no object but he had forgotten one thing although he was up to the minute with market trends, he did not reckon with the recession just around the corner, that it would be knocking on his door before he realised it.

John blurted out to his wife his financial state one Sunday morning.

They had got up and Liz was buttering toast for herself. She turned and looked at him.

'Am I hearing properly, are you sure?'

She sat down at the kitchen table, her breath coming in little gasps as the full force of his words registered.

'Do you mean honestly that this house has to go to square up the bank?'

John turned and looked out at the overgrown garden.

'Yes it has and other things as well,' he said.

'Other things. What other things? Please tell me, this cannot be happening.' her voice all of a sudden becoming croaky.

Liz had been talking to his back but as she stopped speaking he slowly turned, his face ashen. For a few seconds she stared at him, the torment was there to be seen. Instead of thirty-nine, he looked sixty-nine. Liz knew deep down how much it had cost him, to tell her the full details.

'The downhill road started around eighteen months ago and it has steadily got worse.' confessed John.

For a long moment it was his turn to look at Liz. Her face slumped into her hands, elbows on the table, dejected and isolated. He took one step and fell on his knees putting his arms around her holding her tightly. A tear escaped and ran down her cheek. At length they clung together their emotions intermingled, the real world suspended for the moment.

Days passed quicker than they liked. Instead of things turning to their advantage they could not see a glimmer of hope. Liz seemed to be the stronger of the two when they were facing the worst time of their lives.

They had been over the plight they had found themselves in again and again. Discriminations had been voiced from both of them. Liz saying lots of things that weren't called for, hurtful and damning innuendoes, but once said she felt better getting them off her chest. As for John, when roused, hit where it felt most. Liz could not stop his tirade, she covered her ears until he drew breath. It was useless to try and appease him.

Official looking letters had come through the letterbox and they had been put to one side.

'I shall open them later.' John had said.

Liz had found a score of these at the back of the bureau and now started to open them. Everyone was a demanding letter from solicitors on behalf of their clients. The last two, she was horrified, they were hotels they had stayed at in Buckinghamshire for three weeks and eight days respectively away in November of last year. She remembered only too well both were full board and looking at the amounts, she could hardly believe the staggering figure. Liz prowled around the house like a demented lioness.

'Where the devil is he?'

She could not contain herself. She grabbed her coat and ran out of the front door. It seemed as she ran she put a wide birth between herself and the awful truth she had just discovered.

Liz nose-dived into John on the bend of the drive. John catching her left arm swinging her round to a stop seeing her blazing eyes.

'Steady on. Nothing can be as bad as you make out.'

Liz gathered strength from somewhere. She pummelled his chest with her fists.

'Typical! I don't know how you can be so placid. Do you know what is in those letters in the bureau? Don't tell me you have forgotten about them. All of them are demanding money and you have the audacity to tell me nothing can be as bad as I make out.'

John was floored for a second then he gathered himself.

'I will see to them. There must be a mistake. We hardly could have incurred all that debt.'

The shrill ringing of the telephone could be heard as they entered the house again.

'You answer it.' John motioned to Liz.

'No I'm not, it will be for you.' said Liz shaking her head at John.

Even now she was thinking something or someone would spark off the rumour of John's demise.

He picked up the receiver. His father bellowed down the line.

'How are you both?'

Liz saw John's face light up. He came off the phone looking pleased.

'Dad is coming next weekend. He is not bringing Mother this time, he thought it was best and I did tell him about us.'

'What did he say? Did he not hit the roof?' Liz asked.

'More puzzled than anything.' John replied.

Liz always looked forward to seeing John's parents and got on well especially with his father. Every time they came they spent an hour retailing what had gone on in the village. This was really for John's benefit although by now she had got to know who they were talking about and inevitably one or the other would say, 'no sign of the patter of little feet.'

This used to hurt Liz but not anymore.

Father and son sat well into the night trying to work out the best way around their problem. Liz had gone to bed exhausted, the two men determined to thrash it out and find a solution before going upstairs. Next morning Liz was told the outcome of their deliberations. It was father who was going to come to the rescue. He was going to settle up the mounting debt.

Liz could not have been more relieved at this juncture, but father knowing his son like the back of his hand, no doubt about it, had not lived with him these past years. His son had taken risk after risk. These risks had paid off but had taken Liz nearly to the brink of a nervous breakdown. In the past John's parents were oblivious to their son's living on a knife-edge.

If they had known the full facts Liz thought the outcome would be very different.

With transactions at John's bank seen to, father had gone home. He had come to Liz on the morning of his departure.

'Bye Liz, don't worry now. I have straightened John up and he assures me he wont get into that mess again. I must say though I cannot apportion all the blame to him, it is the world we live in.'

Whether it had been the world economy at that moment or not which had brought John to this catastrophic state, even now Liz had an uneasy feeling. This feeling stayed with her as if another bubble would burst at any time and knock their legs from under them.

John was in limbo, marking time although time had moved on.

Six months had gone by. At first John was full of plans eager to get going.

It was just a little hiccup he said one day but he hadn't got going again. He was becoming withdrawn. Liz had seen the change very gradually.

At first she put it down to being over cautious. That in itself was pleasing to Liz but it was becoming hard and a problem for her to talk to him. He would flare up at the least thing.

'You don't know the half of what I am feeling at this moment.'

He would jump up from his chair and storm out and be gone for hours. Sometimes he would come back having had a chat with a neighbour. Although only acquaintances they passed the time of day more frequently.

This played on John's imagination when the neighbours were out of sight and they got the full force of his tongue. Things had to come to a head.

Liz was more than thankful when John let slip that one such fellow had come up to him and offered his shoulder to lean on. He knew exactly what John was going through. One minute full of optimism the next floundering hardly knowing which way to turn. It was inevitable that John should go and file his petition for bankruptcy. If he didn't, ' the vultures' would do it for him said his friend. Surely it hadn't come to this. They were aware of father clearing up the debts but with no regular income at the end of the month something had to be done but, oh no, not that.

Liz tentatively asked what John would say to Harry if they saw him and made an appointment. In the past John had never given a thought to businesses, individuals who were on the slippery slope where money was concerned. Most probably he would have taken the view that they should have seen it coming and they deserved everything that was coming to them.

It would never have run through his head to think 'poor blighters.'

'I'll have to tell him everything. I won't mention about the old boy rescuing us if I can help it.'

'Now then your father wouldn't like you referring to him like that John and besides don't you think Harry will have heard from some source, your predicament. You know bankers and solicitors move around in the same circles and you don't mean to tell me they don't talk amongst themselves.' concluded Liz.

They were both in limbo often sitting for hours each day. John looking far into the distance, his eyes blind to the view. Liz had started reading her old diary, immersing herself, lost was the present. Liz was living the past, so amazed at the things that she was reading between the diary pages.

One entry was their time spent in Paris. They had motored down and left the car in Dover and boarded the Sea Link to Calais. Liz remembered how they had stood by the rail watching the famous white cliffs receding into the distance. The sun high in the sky. The channel a blue green and the mass of water being cut open by the thrust of the boat churning up huge white billowy froth, leaving a distinct trail behind it.

How vivid the time spent in Paris now was. Her eyes misted over. John loved her and Liz loved him in those days but now, they seemed to be pulling apart. Liz pushed away the awful thought near the surface. They were nearly at the pitch of hating each other instead of facing the next weeks in the knowledge that they would get through whatever was facing them.

She turned the page again and Liz at once was drawn in to the sights and sounds of Paris. The music, the wide squares, the Eiffel Tower. The first evening on a tour of the city was breathtaking, twinkling lights, myriads of them. Going around the Arc de Triomphe and Notre Dame. Suddenly the velvet sky ripped open by a jagged blue electric light zigzagging down to earth. Cocooned in the warmth of the limousine, looking through the side windows, seeing the Parisians, the whole population of Paris it seemed charging to the overhangs of the many monuments, sheltering out of the drenching rain. The deluge was unstoppable. The French Eye visible to all Paris lit up relentlessly. It was stubborn almost as if it were putting on a performance for the stotting, splashing rain.

Chapter 2

Liz came down with a bump.

'Are you listening to me damn it, are you?' said John.

John had risen from his chair and now he was leaning on the table looking down at her. It was the first time in a long while Liz had seen him with that air of resolve about him. Even the choice of words to her did not matter as in the past when he came to a decision either made solely by him or jointly, he raised his voice as if to clarify and pin down his statements.

'Come on, get your coat we are going to see Harry.'

'Should we telephone him first?' asked Liz.

'We will go on speck. He'll see us if he is there and not away.'

Harry came out of the inner sanctum looking pleased to see them but a little puzzled.

'How are you both?' he greeted them.

Those same words had been bellowed down the telephone by his father. John remembered.

Harry led the way and showed them into his rooms.

'How can I be of assistance?' he asked.

He motioned them to sit down on the two high-backed chairs on the other side of his desk.

'Well Harry we have come for advice on what to do. It is becoming difficult for us to make ends meet and we really need you to put us in the right direction.' John said.

'Business not good at present then? I do know some properties are standing still.' said Harry.

John and Liz nodded in unison.

'I never understood Liz and John, why you took the property you live in off the market six months ago. Can you tell me why you withdrew it?'

'I'll answer that.' said Liz. 'You can remember Harry? I rang up about it. John did tell me about the house being put on the market but at the time I had grown fond of the old place, the locality, the situation. It is the only house I have lived in for any space of time. All the other properties we never lived in for long. I never questioned why it was put on the market. If I had only asked I realise now we would not be in this awful position. I was angry too and the only thing on my mind was to stop the sale.'

Harry considered what they had divulged. The simple fact was they were running out of hard cash.

'There are two ways to ease the cash flow. Put the house on the market again, no quibbling and hope you get some one that is interested in the property and will pay the asking price or near enough, though property is at a low. In these circumstances your name John will stand for something.'

They nodded at Harry in agreement.

'The second option,' continued Harry, 'is to move out and let the property. It is a substantial house in a lovely part of the country. The types of people looking for a house like yours to let are the managers in the local town that are just here for four or five years and then move on elsewhere.'

'Would we get someone like that?' asked Liz anxiously.

'Of course you would, no bother at all.' said Harry rubbing his chin.

'I know someone who is looking to rent. Could you move and find somewhere in a month?'

At this point John had not spoken for sometime letting Liz hold the floor.

'Hold on a minute. I think the best thing we can do is mull over what you have suggested and then we will get back to you and tell you one way or another.'

'That will be excellent. I don't want to push or hurry you but I think the state of play points that way doesn't it?' concluded Harry.

John and Liz took their leave. Liz voiced her thoughts as they got out of the car at home.

'I would love to keep this.' This being the house.

John looked at the old house as he came round the bonnet of the car and paused before starting for the front door.

'I know Liz, but I cannot see how we could keep it. No we will have to sell it. How could we live with out selling? No it has to go.'

They fell silent, both resigned to the fact that selling was the best option.

Two days later the telephone rang. Liz jumped at the shrill ring. It had lain quiet for days. It was Harry.

'I've got a proposition for you. Is John there?'

'He's gone for a walk Harry. He should be back before too long 'said Liz.

'I wonder if you and John could come down to see me? I would not ask but I think it will be to your advantage.'

Time was set for the afternoon. When Liz hung up the telephone she was left wondering what Harry and his proposition was as he didn't give her an inkling. John had to be there when it was broached and voiced again.

It was an anxious time for both of them but John seemed to be more tense. He came into the house and Liz told him of the phone message from Harry.

'Why can't he come and see us for once and what will he have to say to us? You know we pay heavily when his account comes in.' grumbled John.

Liz stared at him aghast, her eyes blazing.

'Oh you are the limit. You should be ashamed of yourself. Harry is only trying to help us. Can't you ever think how lucky we are to have a solicitor like Harry. You know few solicitors are there to help and advise in this case. It would be a different story if you were to be faced with your bank manager. He would want to know the ins and outs. You are so ungrateful and it is uncalled for. At least Harry has not probed too far.'

When John was so unreasonable Liz wished she were miles away. Even someone she could talk to would give her light relief but there was no one.

They arrived at Harry's office. He was waiting for them.

'Something has come up. I would like to hear your comments. I had intimation from the Innes Estate. Do you know of it?' said Harry.

'We have heard of it, haven't we Liz? We have driven past it a few times but that is all.' said John.

Harry had a letter in front of him. He pointed to it.

'It is a working estate and intact. A home farm and six other farms round about. It once had a racing stable but that was sold. Lady Innes I believe used to be the main one at the stables until she met with an accident.'

John looked at Liz at this point and then said to Harry.

'I cannot see where we come in. I can't see us fitting in anywhere on the estate.'

'That is where you are wrong,' said Harry. 'What I want to hear from you, would you be interested in the position of caretaker at the big house?'

John was taken aback. Liz too raised her eyebrows. They sat not uttering a word. Then Harry broke the silence.

'Lady Innes died six months ago and the whole estate is willed to a nephew. He is in America. He has no use for the estate now.'

'Is the estate coming on the market then?' asked John.

'No. There is no question of it going under the hammer. The Innes family is a large one.' said Harry.

Harry paused looking at them both questioningly.

'I see that you are a little baffled. I don't blame you. I imagine what you are thinking. You could not even entertain the possibility of going down there and living on an estate.'

He opened a drawer in his desk and drew out a large envelope.

'I want you to read these details and then get back to me.'

They took their leave, John throwing the details into the back of the car.

'Who does he think we are, I ask you?' muttered John.

Liz knew he was mad by his manner, ramming the car into reverse and shooting out of the parking space nearly hitting an oncoming van.

'Be careful John, please watch where you are going.'

'If he thinks that we are----.' he tailed off.

Liz did not say anything at this point, she wanted to see the details for herself and peruse them carefully that evening.

A damp drizzle started as they headed out of town and as they neared home a steady down pour was making the car wheels swish along the wet roads.

Liz busied herself with making the supper. Both she and John were deep in thought. At least Liz knew that John had taken the envelope and there was no noise from the television coming from the sitting room so he must be looking at it.

After tidying up the supper dishes Liz settled down with the details. It was a hefty bit of literature. In side the covers were three contained, almost like catalogues. The first one there was a photograph of the big house itself.

It looked magnificent. It was set in parkland and had been taken on a glorious sunny day. Well documented, features showing pictures of notable bedrooms and marble halls.

The second dealt with the farms and cottages. The farms were too large to comprehend so a map showing the boundaries was attached to each one.

The last, but not least of these, showed the village hall, the church, the school and the tiny shop. Copious notes followed each section.

Liz was exhausted trying to take in everything written about the Innes Hall Estate. Discussing it with John that night was hopeless. He was dead against even going to see it.

A week later having been persuaded by Harry to go with him to see the estate, they turned in at the main gates. Travelling through the parkland the house could be seen at a distance. The sun dappled the ground, its rays piercing the network of branches and leaves and glinting on the car and drive ahead. As they moved the house seemed to be drawing nearer but suddenly it went out of sight appearing when they had negotiated a wide sweeping bend and a hump backed bridge. John let out a low whistle. His spirits rose visibly. Even he could not but appreciate the grandeur of the mansion towering and dwarfing the three as they got out of the car.

The next week was hectic. Harry had sent an S.O.S. to be at home on Thursday. He had found a family that would be suitable to take over the tenancy of their property.

'That was quick.' said John.

He had come in from tidying the garden and pruning some of the straggly plants and shrubs near the house.

'Yes, but do you know what this means. We'll have to vacate in double quick time if they like it and surely they will. No one would go away from the house and the location having a bad impression.' ended Liz.

True to their word a shabby old Saab drew up at the front door on Thursday lunchtime. A father, a mother and six children tumbled out of the car. One let out a squeal of delight and made for the big old gnarled oak tree. His father grabbed him by the shoulder.

'Remember where you are.' he said to his straining son.

The son stopped in his tracks but not for long. He was intent on climbing the old tree. His father let go of him and he darted across the lawn, the others tearing after him.

John and Liz had seen the little scene out of the dining room window.

'My! The old house will get a shock if they decide to settle here.' said John glancing at Liz.

Gathering her hand in his, Liz was aware of a change in John. Twice he had caught hold of her hand this morning. She raised her eyebrows. He must be feeling like the old John she knew but even then she slightly stiffened at his touch.

The family was like a dozen others. As well as a shabby car they were shabby too. Their clothes were ill fitting but brightly coloured. Mother was plump and wore a faded blue smock belted round the waist. She had big flat sandals on her bulging feet but when one saw her face it was serene and happy. It passed through Liz's mind, "Keep hold of her." Her husband was a lucky, lucky man. The children were a cross between mother and father. Only one was father's double, the boy who was straining to climb the tree.

John and Liz went down the two steps to greet them. They showed the family the back and front gardens of the property and then they took them down the side of the house that led to the river.

'Is it deep in parts?' asked the mother, uncertain for a moment.

'It is shallow and hard bottomed, nothing to worry about. If it is the children you are concerned about playing in and out of the river there is no need.' said John putting her mind at rest.

As they turned and started to climb the little incline to the house, the mother let out a gasp.

'Oh Peter this is just what I imagined it would be.'

She was seeing it at a different angle altogether. The solid looking house was welcoming and beckoning to the viewers to come up the steps to the open door. The children for a space were out of sight but were heard by their screeches and laughter under the old oak and their running in and out of the low shrubs and rough ground. The parents wandered around the house. It was seen that they appreciated the wide spaces it contained. The family had lived in a cramped area for so long.

'The house is just what we are looking for.' said the husband.

The mother after being told they were on a bus route, called the children and they piled into the car and waved good-bye.

come in from sideshows and a case selling fine and expensive perfumes had bumped up the takings enormously. She and John had seen the nephew to the airport and now they were slumped on the sofa.

'I am exhausted. I don't know about you but I have never worked as hard in my life. If this is putting on a lunch and all the trimmings, I am glad it happens only once a year.' concluded John.

'I am tired too,' said Liz. 'but happy in the knowledge that everything went off o.k. and the visitors who gave money for the tickets enjoyed the lunch.'

The following day saw the firm that had brought the round tables, come and stack them in a big van and take them away in two lots. By three o'clock the hall was back to normal showing the vast expanse of black and white tiles stretching to the foot of the grand staircase. The flowers at the foot of the stairway were left as a reminder of the day before. The flowers lasted well over a week until the gardener came and took the big vases away. Even he had been pleased with the amount the greenhouses had produced.

Liz took time out to walk in the grounds and follow the meandering river. She loved these quiet moments. Each time she went into the parkland she could not but feel a lightening of her spirits. Liz kicked off her shoes when it was dry underfoot and felt the short green grass where the sheep had cropped it down to a smooth lawn. She breathed in the fresh country clear air as she slowly walked by the river's edge. Today the river was dappled with sunlight and in parts, below the surface of the water, the long strands of weed bobbed up and down. Liz liked coming here as it reminded her of the stretch of water flowing past the bottom of their garden at home. She thought of the occupants fleetingly, then the rock where she had made decisions of utmost importance, the moment when she had made the decision not to sell their house and John being furious when he had heard what she had done. She mused at the hundred and one incidents that had come and gone since then. Liz glanced at her watch as she turned and made her way back. She found herself not far from where the ground gave way with the little stone bench at the top end inviting her to pause a while. This day someone else was sitting on the bench. She hesitated and half turned away but involuntarily turned back to see a man rising to his feet. He raised his hand and came towards her.

'I'm sorry to be trespassing,' he said, 'but I come to this spot every year. I was sitting here on this slab when you first came.'

Liz was taken aback at this and wondered why this man and his whereabouts were not talked of at the beginning. They had been given a list of names who worked at the Hall, but no mention of this man was recorded. Liz did not question why he was here but said to the stranger.

'I shall see you again maybe when I am out and about.' she smiled and left him.

Surreptitiously she glanced over her shoulder and saw he had moved back to the bench. Something checked her telling John about her brief encounter with him when she eventually opened the door into their apartment.

'I have been looking for you. I am thinking of going up to see father. Would you mind?' asked John.

'This is sudden isn't it?' said Liz.

'Yes but if I have a few days away now, I'll be here when you go on holiday.' he replied.

'Well it is impossible for me to have a break until the end of the season. When are you hoping to journey up there?' asked Liz.

'I thought I would start off to-morrow if that is all right with you. I think Dad needs me to fill in forms and the garden has given him a few aches. He has been working too hard, but he told you all this over the telephone didn't he?'

'There is one thing John, we shall have to visit the stables when you get back. They are expecting us. There hasn't been an opportunity since the charity event, but Denise was in touch this morning telling us not to forget and plan an afternoon to drive over there. They are eager to show us the horses they have stabled there and have in training.'

'Yes I have been thinking about them and when we could fit them in. The trouble is the time just flies and the weeks quickly move into months. I saw Edward only this morning, when I was turning in at the gate and he was making his way to town.

Chapter 6

John set off in the four by four next day leaving the small car for Liz.

'I'll ring when I get there.' said John.

Three ladies had come from the village to help Liz with the drawing-room curtains. They met John half way down the drive. He gave them a wave as he negotiated his way passed their car.

'He's in a hurry. He nearly swiped our nose off.' said the lady who had hold of the wheel. She of course was referring to the car's bonnet and she said below her breath that surely we were on our right side. The other two occupants gave out a little gasp. She did feel her cheeks go a little pink though but she straightened up the car and drove on.

There were five large windows in the drawing room from floor to ceiling. The curtains had to be taken down one by one. The hangings were a rich heavy fabric with a silky finish woven with a raised pattern offset by gold, the main colour being red. The brocade was saved from the sun's rays by the linings. These linings had to be inspected meticulously as in all the rooms facing south. The sun was no respecter of objects or fabrics and not inspected regularly the linings would rot away and harm the curtains.

One of the gardeners went up the ladder and unhooked them. He came down the ladder each time where a lady was waiting with outstretched arms to catch the single curtain. This took time but when he had completed his task and gone, the helpers spread out each curtain on the floor with the linings being uppermost.

It all depended how many linings had to be replaced and how long it would take. In the sewing room a bolt of lining material was kept over from one season to the next so nothing hindered the three sewing ladies tackling their work in hand. The Hall was open on a Wednesday and the weekends. Times were fixed at the very beginning of the season so everyone knew where she stood. If a curtain had been overlooked and brought to the attention of Liz, it was taken down and mended on the days they were closed.

John had been home a week when he and Liz started off for the stables. Nestling to the left of the long lane, the house snug amongst the shrubs and lawns, the car turned in at the gate and came to a halt at the front door. They got out of the car to be greeted by Edward and Denise.

'So good to see you both at last,' said their hosts.

They moved to the front door and Edward said.

'Mind the lintel, you can get a mighty crack on the head if you are not careful.'

He was used to the low swung house and doors. Visitors if not warned quickly enough were brought up sharply. The two men went along the short passage to the sitting room while Denise and Liz headed for the kitchen.

Edward was a tall man with prematurely white hair. This added to his attraction. He was a no nonsense type. He spoke his mind and did not suffer fools gladly. He had married Denise after meeting her at a Spring Sale. She had something in common with him, the horse, but nothing else. She lived in a remote village in Cornwall and worked in the summer at a trekking establishment, helping with the horses and taking out riders on the moors. Meeting Edward was a one off, never dreaming that she would meet the man that she would marry, let alone land up at Newmarket in the first place.

Edward and Denise had no children but when schools were closed for the summer, nephews and nieces were to be found at the stables. Edward and Denise were not averse to the odd squabble or to high spirits. Even to the " I know better." attitude of the youth. It was the process of growing up that was all. Soon they would settle in and appreciate living at a racing stable.

As for Denise no one could pass her by without a smile or a cheery hello. Husband and wife worked as a team and with Denise, Edward was ever grateful for her assistance. She brought a warmth to the stables and saw that the stable boys and girls were happy in their work. Anything they wanted or wondered if they could ask, and they did ask, they went to Denise. At nine in the morning

Denise went into the office. Her job was to answer messages on the answer phone, then get in touch with clients whose horses were in their care, either to give them a progress report or to give them a calendar of races which their individual horses would enter. It was a busy life but it was their life. Nothing would change it, they were committed. Edward and Denise knew nothing else.

Denise went over to the Aga and opened the warming oven. She pulled out a baked salmon already on its platter. She removed the tin foil.

'Oh what a wonderful sight! A whole salmon,' said Liz.

Denise took the main dish into the dining room and placed it on the table. The table was set with several mixed salads and Denise sprinkled these with a touch of oil. Cold sweets were already on the sideboard with cheese and biscuits.

Liz went for the two men along the passage. Edward immediately got up and came to her.

'Can I pour you a sherry?' he asked.

'No, but thank you. We are needed in the dining room.'

They sat down. Each couple had got to know each other well enough that conversation flowed easily.

'How long have you had the stables? I believe they belonged to the estate. Am I right? ' enquired John.

'We have been here nearly eight years, come the autumn,' said Edward. 'Denise and I were employed by Lady Innes until she took a back seat. Then she had the accident.'

'We heard you had bought it some time ago,' said Liz.

Edward and Denise nodded. Denise carried on then.

'It was an awful shock when Lady Innes had her accident. We thought we would have her valuable advice for years but you see, one can never tell from one minute to the next.'

Edward told them how one evening she had been out at a friend's house and was returning to the Hall, when a deer bumped into her car. It was winter and the roads had a smattering of snow on them. Lady Innes was coming up the drive when the accident occurred. The deer jumped out on a blind corner and hit the side of the vehicle and slewed it around. Lady Innes lost control of the wheel momentarily but gained the steering again. The result was worse than expected. Lady Innes heard her leg snap. Being that much older her leg never healed as it should. One of the gardeners found her in the morning when he was coming to work. He raised the alarm and soon she was being taken to the hospital in the ambulance. It was touch and go at first. She had been there all night. Lady Innes must have had a strong bit about her, she could have easily succumbed to the bitter cold. She was never free of her stick after that.

After lunch they talked some more in the sitting room and then Edward and Denise took John and Liz up to the stables. They followed the lane for half a mile and then facing them, the stables came into view. The building was imposing. Passing beneath the clock tower it opened into a vast yard. It was wide and square. The horseboxes were built around this square. In the middle of the area a fountain played. Water spurted to the heavens then cascaded down to a large round, pool. There was much activity. Although the gallops had been done in the early morning, stable lads were bringing in young horses to get them used to being handled and groomed.

'In the winter months, if your horse or horses are up to their hocks in mud, watch out. It can easily lead to lameness. The complaint is called mud fever.' said Edward. 'If some of them here get it, we wash them with disinfectant. If they are out in the fields for any length of time and they roll in the mud, which they are prone to do, well that is what happens. It is a problem. You cannot win.'

John and Liz nodded appreciating the fact and realising how much hard work goes into the running of a stable and the calibre of this one. They walked over to the far side of the yard to the gate with Denise while Edward brought over the land rover. He was going to show them the gallops. John got in the front and Liz and Denise piled in the back. It was an all weather gallop. As the land rover moved slowly along the track, the ground got steeper, giving way to clumps of gorse bushes on the left, on the other the beginning of a dense wood. As the vehicle gathered speed, row upon row of trees climbed with them. Turning their eyes to the right, through the darkness of the trees, bright lights flitted in quick succession like a camera shooting a sequence of pictures. Abruptly the shutter ceased to function leaving the mass of dark green wood behind them. Changing gear and still climbing further Edward drove the land rover on to a perfect plateau. The party got out and surveyed the landscape. Up here one could see on a fine clear day a patchwork quilt of greens, yellows and browns broken only by farm steadings surrounded by the odd clump of trees shielding them from the winter blasts.

'Isn't it breath taking.' said Denise as she came up to Liz. She pointed out different areas of interest to Liz, especially further a field than Liz thought possible, Innes Hall stood, solidly built on a mound, keeping a watchful eye on the undulating countryside.

'I have never seen such a panoramic view as this in years.' said Liz spreading her arms wide to denote the huge picture she was contemplating.

She marvelled at the vastness. To the south the land ran down and levelled out to a rolling plain. To the north, east and west the land gave up its richness in the form of waving wheat, corn and barley, nodding in unison with each other. A silver blue snake ran through the land petering out behind the odd steading to reappear further in the distance. The road they had come on a mere track. Up here nearly touching the clouds, it was a different world. The sun shone fiercely. The slightest of breezes played on their upturned faces and looking down again from their vantage point, dairy cows were grazing on luscious green grass.

A droning became louder and louder and involuntarily Liz ducked as two menacing planes flew over their heads in practise. Down at Innes Hall planes were often heard but they never sounded so deafening as these two had just done. Looking after them they flew straight across the countryside then arched themselves as if they were lying on their sides, the drone giving way to a screech. Soon there was no sound, no vibration in the sky. The planes were minute specks in the far distance. Edward started up the engine and the party continued across the plateau, turning left and down the opposite side until they ended up at the yard gate from where they had started.

'I saw red and white cattle as we drove up the gallops. Do they belong to you Edward or do they belong to the farmer next door?' asked John.

'They belong to Denise, John. Lady Innes always had a batch. We have carried on where she left off.'

'Do you sell them at a particular time then, or do you keep them for good?' asked John. Denise and Liz were immediately behind the two men.

'The five stirks you saw will be sold to the next door farmer.' Said Denise. She continued. 'We knew Lady Innes had an arrangement with him. She sold her cattle to him, so now he takes our animals. It has worked out well. We buy them in the spring and let them go in about October or November. Edward and I would like two cows and their followers next year, but it will depend on what is on offer at the time.'

John nodded, and said, 'Quite.'

They crossed the yard skirting the fountain and came to the clock tower.

'I won't be a minute. I am popping into the office. I'm expecting a fax. Coming John?' said Edward heading off in the direction of the office. John followed.

'We'll start walking home then.' said Denise. 'You will probably catch us up.'

As they walked enjoying the beautiful day Liz said-

'What a great place you have here.'

'Yes it is, isn't it?' Denise smiled. 'When Lady Innes decided to sell the racing stables, she came to us and offered us first refusal. At the time, we had some doubting moments wondering whether we would be able to keep going. Of course now looking back, we are glad we did. We are still maintaining the high standard that Lady Innes attained and we have the good horses coming in to be trained. Luckily too, the then clients knew my husband. It wasn't as if he was a new trainer and when he was Lady Innis' right hand man he worked wonders with her horses.'

'One can see he is so keen about every aspect, the horses above all else and the buildings that are housing the horses. Is he going to extend over there?' Liz pointed to the right of the yard.

'He is hoping to build and update the bunkhouse with facilities, so some of the lads can stay overnight when they are racing the next day.' answered Denise.

'Is that a digger then?' asked Liz glancing back to the buildings.

'Yes it is and you can't see them, but at the back of the buildings we had a delivery of rubble to firm up the foundations. Edward is anxious to get started on it.'

'He will have his hands full, knowing how busy he is without the building.' declared Liz.

Denise smiled at what Liz had just been saying.

'Yes but he likes to improve the stables as much as he can and this, he thinks is an improvement.'

They walked on in companionable silence, then Denise spoke.

'You know Liz, Edward was brought up watching his father break horses at home in County Wexford. He hunted where at all possible when he wasn't at school and he was a natural on horseback. He wanted nothing more than to work with horses.'

'Born in the saddle, so the saying goes.' said Liz looking at Denise who nodded appreciatively.

'Did he come over to England after leaving school, or did he stay with and learn more from his father?' asked Liz.

'No he didn't stay with his father, but he advised Edward to join Paddy Slattery's yard and then Pat O' Malley's yard where he spent three years riding and working. It was then he came to England and spent time as a jockey, then assistant trainer with Pat Fitzgerald moving on to David Pattinson's stable to complete his experience.'

'When did he become fully fledged then as a trainer?' said Liz.

'It didn't take long. Coming from Ireland with an excellent curriculum vitae and references, Edward started as the trainer here. The rest you know. Look, we have beaten the men arriving home first, let me show you the garden before we go in and have a cup of tea.' Denise finished.

Denise opened the side wicket and let Liz pass her, holding the gate so it did not swing quickly behind her. As they went along the path, the air hung heavy with the scents of the herbaceous border and the constant drone of the honeybees busily gathering nectar from the flowers. The mid-day sun had shifted its gaze and left parts of the garden deep in shadow only to be found shining at a reasonable quarter past four on the sundial. The shrubbery having been well established at the bottom of the stretch of lawn shielded the house and the numerous colours of green in the shrubbery provided sharp contrast, against the ice blue of the sky. They came to a summerhouse partly sheltered but exposed to the evening sun. It had a veranda at the front. Stepping up on to the platform that surrounded three sides, they entered a good-sized sitting area with an assortment of chairs round a wooden table. Stacked up against the wall were deck chairs and in the corner with the lid missing, a croquet set which had seen better days. One could sit and view the distant hills or immediately the rose bed but not doing the latter, one could pick up a hoe. It was a useful place to house the garden tools and the lawn mower. As they were coming out and shutting the door, Denise caught sight of the land rover going into the yard at the back.

'Oh, they are here Liz. We'll go through the main lobby.' said Denise, opening the front door.

Edward and John turned as they came into the kitchen. Edward had been filling the kettle and putting it on the Aga. It gave out a sizzling sound as it hit the hotplate.

'Sorry we have been a little longer than anticipated. I had two faxes waiting for me. One wasn't urgent but the second one, I had to fax a reply straight away concerning a forthcoming race next week. The owner was worried if his horse would be up to it.' said Edward.

'I suppose that is a problem in some cases.' said Liz. 'But surely most of the owners will leave that to you Edward?'

'Oh yes, but they do get anxious and nervous, some of them.' said Edward.

The four of them sat round the kitchen table drinking their tea.

'This afternoon has just been great.' John turned to Edward.

'It must be hard work getting up so early, but I see the rewards far outweigh any disappointments that you might have.'

John and Liz took their leave, Liz glancing at her watch and finding, it was later than she thought.

Chapter 7

'Who is that?' said Liz.

Looking out of the sitting room window, she saw a pretty red head climbing out of a posh sporty looking car. Her face upturned looking at the house. John moved to the window. Liz could not but see his expression as he glanced down at the girl, recognition dawning on his face.

'Who is she?' Liz said again.

John brushed passed her not giving any explanation. He opened and banged the door behind him not meaning to slam it so loudly and for a moment, he could not think how he would put over plausibly to Liz, who the girl was and why she had arrived here in the first place.

Being Liz, she was as astute as John in some things. She remembered way back, the girl had been at his mother's funeral. John had spent practically all afternoon with her but he never brought her over and introduced her to Liz. The girl seemed to be fond of John's father. Liz assumed she had lived in the village all her life.

John straightened his tie as he opened the outer door and went round the side of the house to the front. The red head saw him and strode towards him.

'Oh John I have missed you.'

He held her at arms length.

'Angela, why did you come here of all places?' said John angrily.

'Why not? I cannot go on like this. I want to be with you always. You promised.' Angela's voice was rising considerably.

'I know I did, but I must take it slowly. Liz does not know anything about us.' said John.

Angela turned blazing eyes on him.

'I thought, I understood you told her months ago. Why didn't you?'

'Angela, it wasn't the right time.'

'But John I have come to be with you. I am not going home.' she said emphatically, clutching an over night case in her hand.

John caught hold of her shoulder and steered her in the direction of her car.

'Don't shout will you. Liz can see you. She is at the window.'

He opened the passenger door and motioned her to get in. He moved to the driving seat and started up the engine. He reversed and turned the low slung car and shot over the gravel gathering speed and made for the driveway.

'Where are we going?' Angela shouted, frantically trying to find her seat belt. 'Don't drive like a maniac.'

' If you had thought and had some sense I wouldn't be driving like, as you say, a maniac. I want you as far away as possible until I get Liz sorted out.' John finished.

It was a full minute before Angela gave vent. She got hold of the wheel and screamed to stop the car. Somehow John got hold of her hand and prized it off the wheel.

'Don't be stupid, you could cause an accident doing that. You could end up in hospital, then what?' said John.

Angela slumped back in her seat, realising the enormity of her actions.

Liz moved from the window and sat down heavily on the sofa. She had seen John drive away with the girl in her car. 'Now what!' she said to the quiet room. She pondered on the scene that she had witnessed a few minutes ago. Although from the sitting room window she could not hear anything that was said, Liz did catch a glimpse of John's face and saw how roughly he moved her away from the sight of the window. Liz might have known though. To be truthful to herself, she knew this would happen sooner or later. She had buried the sight of John and the girl at his mother's funeral. The knowledge of John going up to see his father and staying a few days, she saying one time to him. 'I can't possibly go up while the house is open.' All this was floating round in her head, the red head in the background. Liz's thoughts were interrupted by the telephone. She lifted the receiver to hear John's voice. 'Liz I have been held back. Don't wait up for me. I'll ring you in the morning.' Then the instrument went dead. Liz had been about to say 'Where are you?' but he had hung up. Typical of the man but Liz knew instinctively what was going on and more than that, it made her mind up. Ultimately she would leave him but before that she must speak to Harry and see her position in all this.

Sleep didn't come easily to Liz that night. The past hour had made up her mind. True she fell into bed ready for a good night's sleep but she started thinking of all the obstacles that would come in the way. Stupid little things, even broaching the fact to Denise and Edward when she rang up to thank them for the afternoon they had spent with them only an hour or so ago. She knew she would not mention it to them at this point but lying in bed, toying over things that were just under the surface and others that had lain there for months even years rearing their heads, in the small hours of the morning her brain was alive to the thoughts uppermost and it was possible to mull over clearly what she eventually would do.

At last she got to sleep, only to be awakened at seven in the morning by the alarm clock. After a hurried breakfast she went down stairs and into the great hall and walked across the marble floor, her feet echoing as she went. Liz reached for the key and opened the massive studded door at the front followed by secondary doors to the right, left and back of the Hall. This was done each morning by John, it fell to Liz to do them this morning. Retracing her steps Liz went up the wide impressive staircase. It was climbing it, she noticed for the first time in weeks, the shafts of sunlight dancing on the balustrade. It was in the morning the sun's rays ventured into this part of the Hall. Soon it would move higher in the sky turning its gaze to another part of the building. As Liz stepped on to the landing she started to walk slowly viewing the pictures, grasping the opportunity when it presented itself.

Liz was rushed off her feet the whole day. It started with a call for John. With John not being there, she asked if she could help. After hearing it was a supply of guttering for one part of the roof, Liz said she would get someone to be here when she knew what time the load would arrive. That was around eleven o'clock.

Liz could not have a quiet moment to herself and she realised that if one member of the working team was missing, how it can slow down the whole morning. It took time, even finding a man to tell him what was arriving and at what time. That done, she went to the Hall shop and helped stack shelves with a consignment of slabs of toffee and candy. Later she was back, unwrapping books depicting the Hall and surrounding countryside. These particular books did sell well. Before Liz knew it, the afternoon visitors were piling into their cars, the afternoon practically over. The telephone had been ringing throughout the day but no word or sign of John. John or no John, Liz went to bed that night and 'slept the sleep of the just.' Earlier she had spent time mulling over what she was going to do. With John not putting in an appearance, her mind although made up from the night before, even if there was a little niggling doubt, she was going to ring Harry the next day. She would make an appointment to see him in town, better still to have him down here.

Liz let herself out at the side door and made her way through the grounds and skirted round the statue and out by the wicket into the parkland. She sat down on her favourite bench. No longer puzzled that John's father had never visited them, she realised she would never be able to show him the falling away of the ground at this spot and ask his opinion of what might have caused it. It would be unlikely that he was unaware of his son's meetings with the red head when he visited him, Liz was sure about that. It was no use thinking about father at this stage, it was her position at the Hall and everything concerning her living in this stately home that really should be uppermost in her mind.

It was early still when Liz looked at her watch the following day. Twenty past six. Another ten minutes she said to herself. She had woken to the twittering of the birds and the constant blaring of a cow. The cow had obviously had her calf taken from her by the farmer and she had been placed into the milking herd, the rightful place for her. The morning sun even at this early hour was warm on Liz's back. The mist that had shrouded the park and fields earlier had evaporated and left droplets hanging on the webs that the spider had intricately made. One breath of air, the droplets would fall to the shiny green grass below.

As always it was a busy morning. No messages had been left on the answering machine in the flat but word had come through downstairs that John would be away for sometime. John had talked mainly to the man who was overseeing the guttering job. He had been in the Hall when the telephone rang. The man never thought of telling Liz, there was no need. He would think Liz had been in touch with her husband.

Liz made the appointment with Harry's secretary for a fortnight hence. Harry was on holiday and would be expected in ten days time back in the office. Liz also mentioned that she would see him at the Hall, but if anything came in the way he was to give her a buzz. Before donning a coat, Liz got in touch with the stables, thanking Denise and her husband for the lovely and interesting afternoon John and she had spent with them two days before, then she slipped into the driving seat and started up the engine of the car. Her intentions were to drive to her old home. Not to call in but stop the car further along the road, park and walk down the short lane to the river. Liz took in the expanse of water and looked up the river and saw the boulder where she had done her thinking when problems had to be faced. It was a good move taking the house off the market and letting it, but what was paramount in her thoughts now was her job. She wondered about the nephew. He may not like the idea of her carrying on without John. John would have something to say about the set up --------. Liz stopped herself considering what she should do and what she would like to happen. Harry might suggest waiting and hearing John's side of the story. Up until now, Harry did not know what the appointment was about and in the days ahead she might see John driving up in front of the Hall, in the same car he went away in. It was all supposition but she could not but think about it all the same. Liz took a last look at the river and the boulder. She saw that the branches had stretched themselves and obliterated the end of the house. Only visible was a chimneystack. Turning, she hurried back up the lane. Time can pass quickly when one is lulled by a river, she thought, as she opened the car door.

A number of cars met Liz as she pulled in the side on the drive up to Innes Hall and let them pass. The drivers raised their hands in salute. Hopefully they had bought something either in the shop or from the garden. The gardens had something to offer practically all the year round and any purchase from the vegetable garden, the visitor knew it was fresh and pest free. At last the remaining few cars headed for home but not before Liz heard the unmistakable throb of the sports car. She was at the back of the house but as it got nearer the throb got louder until it braked to a stop and the engine died. Now what. Should she go and meet them and say really what was on her mind? Accept her and shake hands, saying she did believe she had met her at mother's funeral? All this passed through her mind as she went to the front of the house.

John and the red head were nowhere to be seen. This made her think that John had taken her to the side door and up the stairs that way. That was the explanation. Liz couldn't possibly have missed them if they had come the front way, even though the house was vast. She was putting the kettle on to boil in the kitchen having drawn a blank, another one, thinking they would be up here in the flat, why on earth did she think that, when John breezed in. He practically breezed out again only holding up a key which he had unhooked from the back of the kitchen door. He said to Liz,

'Can't stop now, speak to you later.'

Liz had no time to ask the crucial question, where is she? Not only that question but she was wondering when he would speak to her. Looking out of the sitting room window Liz saw him get into the sports car and roar off down the drive minus the red head. Liz was too frustrated at the minute to think straight. It was this weekend that Harry was arriving. John had not given her a chance to voice anything about the meeting let alone to ask where he had been. In one way it was best she thought that they had not talked. She might have told him about the imminent meeting with Harry and all it entailed. He would be stumped with the news knowing him, but not for long. He would lash out and actually make her feel the guilty one. For one brief moment it did cross her mind that the redhead might be a stupid girl with a crush and John was managing to make her see sense. Rightly or wrongly Liz had put up with more than enough and whatever Harry said to the contrary, there was no going back. When facing the end of a marriage it was not easy to dwell on anything else. It was just as well Liz was on the top of everything concerning Innes Hall. She had some good and lovely people to run the Hall alongside her. If she had not these ladies, it would have been a different matter.

John had not returned to the Hall nor had she received a telephone message. Liz this morning was waiting for Harry. She had no word from him so she took it he would be arriving shortly. She did not wait long as she heard footsteps along the lobby to her apartment.

'I thought it would be you,' said Liz, as she went out to greet Harry.

'Yes, I went to the office and one of your helpers directed me up here. How are you and John? I have meant to get down here for a social visit that is. I have never had any time to spend in the gardens and my cousin would like to see the Hall when you are open.'

'You must make time then Harry, and come and see for yourself. As for John and me, we are well, but you must be wondering what the appointment is all about. Come and sit down. Do you take milk in your coffee?'

He took the coffee that Liz held out to him and settled down on the kitchen chair facing Liz on the opposite side of the large table.

'I was wondering, where is John?' Harry asked and 'We men easily get waylaid.' he added.

'Well the point is about John and me. John isn't here and I don't know when he will turn up. I can't tell you honestly if he will be here to-day.'

Liz paused and offered Harry a biscuit and at the same time taking one herself, then she continued.

'I know it will come as a surprise to you but I wanted to tell you, as our position here might alter. I ultimately want a divorce.'

Harry did not say anything at this point only. 'Go on.'

'For a very long time, it was intuition really, I felt that he wasn't always telling me everything and on these occasions he evaded

was inevitable that she should break down and cry but not for one moment think that it was self - pity.

Life at The Hall resumed as normal. If some of the staff had heard or thought there might be a rift between John and Liz, they kept that little bit of information to themselves. It was just that, at the moment with John being away, they were bound to wonder. He would have given a plausible story at the beginning when he telephoned the office the first time. He would leave any major work in the capable hands of the men. The men had to run the estate before he came on the scene so why not now. But as the days grew into weeks, and Harry's visiting was becoming more frequent, the rumours were becoming fact. When Harry arrived, John arrived. Soon it was public knowledge and it was best Harry said, if he spoke to the staff all together.

It was a bombshell to most of them even so, but Harry made them to understand that nothing would change in the immediate future. Their concerns and speculations with regard to their working conditions were unfounded but in the back of their minds, a few pondered the possibility of a change. 'Bound to be' said one of the estate workers. It was out in the open and Liz felt better for it. The indoor staff made no mention of it and John was present most days on the estate. True Liz and John did meet as they went about caring for the fabric inside and outside of Innes Hall. No two people could have been better. Their private life did not in anyway intrude. Liz, once did wonder where John had ensconced the red head but it was a fleeting thought.

As the days went into weeks, Liz was getting used to living alone. Innes Hall was a vast pile when the work force had gone home for the night. Walking up the grand stairway Liz's lighter footsteps took on a whispering noise only to be replaced by a clearer note when walking purposefully down in the great hall. Denise had asked her if she would be all right one night when leaving The Stables. Darkness had come upon them earlier than usual. Looking to the west dark clouds shrouded the distant hills.

'We are in for a real down pour maybe even thunder.' said Edward.

'Take care,' they both said, when they heard she would be alright.

Instead of being nervous, Liz felt safe in the big house. It seemed to keep a watchful eye on the near countryside and she inside it.

It was Denise who had hurried to Innes Hall when Edward and she had heard of the split between John and Liz. Actually it was Edward who first heard of it when he had bumped into John shortly afterwards.

'I had better tell you Edward, Liz and I are going our separate ways.'

John did not proffer any details and the only thing Edward did was clasp John's hand for a moment and say,

'Sorry to hear this John.'

Well what could he say the last time he and Denise saw John and Liz was a matter of days ago when they visited the stables. No one would have thought of an under current lying between them.

'Liz what has happened?' concern in Denise's voice.

Although Liz knew it was right what she was doing, she still felt raw inside and Denise being a friendly face and one who could be relied on, even with their short acquaintance, Liz's top lip quivered and tears were near the surface of her bright eyes.

'Edward came home and told me that he had seen John and that you and he were going your separate ways. Surely not Liz! It must be serious when you have taken this step.' she finished.

Liz nodded and Denise put her arm around her shoulder.

'To you and Edward, you will think it is sudden, but I have been brought to the brink once or twice before but this time, I could not take anymore.' Liz said.

'Who is she? Anyone from around here?' Asked Denise.

'No. No one from around here. She lives in the same village as John's father. I have seen her before. The first time was at his mother's funeral. She grew up in the village and their parents were close friends.'

They were silent for a moment then Denise had the awful thought of maybe finding a friend, only to lose her again so soon.

'You're not moving away?' Denise's voice rose with alarm.

'No I hope not.' Liz stretched out her hand and touched Denise's sleeve. It was her turn to reassure this time.

'Gosh is that the time!' Denise exclaimed. 'I must go. We have some would be clients coming over from Ireland, breaking their journey before travelling on to Edinburgh. Edward's old boss got in touch with us and arranged the visit. They are keen to see the young horses we have in training, and of course the stables as a whole.'

Liz waved Denise goodbye and made her way to the shop to collect the list. The café had done brisk business for the last fortnight and coffee and tea had gone down at an alarming rate. Hence the immediate telephone message to the wholesaler to ask if possible, the order for provisions to the Hall could be sent earlier, if not, the tea and the coffee.

Chapter 8

Next day Liz was driving to town to see Harry, she had been sent a document to read through. It was a straightforward document and she was taking it back, rather than sending it. Occasionally the post wasn't always to be relied on. Only last week, the postmen were going to strike over something or other but thankfully it was diverted. Liz looked at her watch and found she was in plenty of time. She took the scenic road to town, leaving the main road, driving through open countryside. The sun broke through the clouds and everywhere one looked, it was fresh and sparkling after a dreadful thunderstorm earlier in the day. Ahead of her the remains of a rainbow, not now clearly defined, the colours smudging into one another. It must have been a split second when her eyes left the road in front of her, to look at the valley below. It only took that second to crash head on into a lorry, knocking her unconscious.

Waking up in the ambulance, she tried to move her head to say something, but no sound came from her lips. Struggling to move, she seemed to be in a straight jacket. Oblivion came to release her tormented face. Her body was not hers.

Liz surfaced to see eyes peering down at her. She was aware she was in hospital with the racket round about her. Nurses dashing passed her bed, trolleys going at great speeds. The only still things, were the two pairs of eyes looking at her.

'You have decided to come back to us. How are you feeling?'

Both the doctor and nurse were smiling down at her and Liz moved to sit up and prop herself on one elbow.

'Steady now, not too fast. I don't want you to move just yet. I want you to take it slowly. Can you follow my finger?' the doctor asked.

Liz concentrated with her eyes. Up, down, right, left. Still examining her the doctor said.

'If you had been driving faster, I doubt you would not have been so lively. As it is you have come off lightly. But you will not feel the aches and pains for a while. I will see you in the morning. If nothing has altered then you can go home. The nurse will give you something to ease the aches if you are uneasy and can't sleep.' He finished.

The doctor moved away and the nurse tidied the bed.

'You will be ready for a cup of tea and if you are up to it, there is a visitor to see you.' The nurse said smiling as a man appeared behind her.

The nurse moved away allowing Liz to see who it was. Coming closer to her bed, it was Harry. For a moment Liz was baffled.

'How did you get here, how did you know I was here?' she asked him.

'I was driving to the office and I heard on the radio about the accident. When you didn't turn up for the appointment, I telephoned Innes Hall. With hearing the radio and knowing the accident happened on the back road, I came here. I even told them who you were.'

'I am sorry to have caused you so much bother but thank you. What is worrying me now, will they know where I am?' she glanced up at Harry, her eyes looking troubled as she said this.

'No need. When I was waiting in the corridor to see you, I rang Innes Hall to tell them. I took the liberty to get in touch with John too. He did say that I might let him know how you were.' ended Harry.

She let out a sigh of relief. Harry had got in touch with the office and as regards John, of course he would be concerned, even though he had vacated the flat and left Liz alone to fend for herself. Bumping into him nearly every day he was bound to wonder where she had got to.

Liz thought about the lorry driver who had driven into her. She knew for a fact accidents were usually followed up by the police. Harry had told her the lorry driver had been driving with caution and his lorry had come to no harm, only the front bumper being terribly bent and hanging off. The examiner found her vehicle was worse for wear but road worthy. It had been towed away and was in a garage a few streets from the hospital. Liz was pleased all in all. The outcome could have been very different even if she didn't feel up to driving her car home straight away. She would ask one of the gardeners if they would take it back to Innes Hall for her.

'I shall be in touch with the hospital. Don't worry about getting home. I will collect you and take you myself.' Harry smiled down at her.

The nurse came to her bedside with a cup of sweet tea and toast. Harry moved and raised his arm in salute. He turned and was gone.

Liz thought about the accident when she was left alone and the nurse had gone to other patients. How lucky she had been. It could have been so much worse. A few bruises to her body were nothing to be bothered about. Her concussion was the problem the Doctor had said, hence the ex-ray. With the results back from that department, the doctor was satisfied and if all was in order next day and the wooziness had not returned she would be discharged. It had made her think more than once how careful one had to be driving. How stupid and lax one can get. She raised her hand to her hot grazed cheek.

'Yes, it is yourself I am telling. Take more care.' She said audibly to her ex-rays at the bottom of the bed.

One of the gardeners brought back Liz's car. A few innards had to be replaced under the bonnet. As Liz had said to the mechanic at the time, to give it a good overhaul, it had taken longer than she imagined. She felt bereft while it was away. She had not driven it since the accident but the longer she left the garage doors shut, she was horrified to realise the fact she might lose her nerve. That would never do but a little niggling doubt persisted when she ever thought of getting behind the wheel. Nothing like the present with shaky hands she lifted the heavy hasp of the garage door.

Arrangements concerning the divorce, in the weeks ahead took up most of her time. It was the swiftness that caught Liz on the hop. She would far rather have slowed down the process now. She felt she wanted to catch her breath. Harry had said 'take your time over this' at the beginning of the process, but she had been adamant when it had been mentioned. He had to press on. As for John when they had met one time in Harry's apartments, he thought it was ideal.

'The sooner the divorce was finalised the sooner they would be able to get on with life,' said John.

Liz wondered, just for a moment if that were really true in his case. But it must be said, John always landed on his feet whatever the circumstances.

Even a divorce wasn't going to alter that fact. Landing on his feet meant that his girlfriend, and as soon as possible his future wife, was well endowed, having a father who owned two mills that he knew of, near the Yorkshire town of Huddersfield.

Liz had gleaned where John was living when passing under the window of an outhouse. She heard two estate workers chatting about him and where he was living at the present time. John had the good sense to remove his girlfriend far enough away from his workplace and as Liz passed under the window and made her way into the park her spirits rose.

'In a few more weeks I shall be free. Blow John and his girl friend. A new chapter is about to begin.' She murmured to herself.

It was Denise who waved Liz away as the plane took off. It was the end of May. Previous to that she had endured the festive season helping the vicar's wife with the Christmas Fair and helping the band of ladies of the village to decorate the church. She had driven herself to the point of exhaustion. Hence being in a plane winging her away to the Adriatic at this precise moment was a little strange but it held an element of excitement.

The holiday had materialised quickly. She had only time to telephone Harry of her intended fortnight away from Innes Hall. To have a word with the ladies that she would be away for that time, and as for Edward and Denise, they thought it a great idea. Edward had said in passing that she deserved it after all that had passed and having Denise near, Liz knew she could unburden herself, and the occasion did arise, if her day hadn't been as straight forward as she had hoped and some technicality concerning the divorce had reared its head. True Liz knew that the past months had taken their toll, even though she had nothing to blame herself for in the slightest. It was the realisation of being completely alone. It would take a little time to adjust to her new life. It wouldn't be easy but she must look at it as a challenge.

Liz strapped herself into her seat and waited for the thrust of the engines to gather speed. She looked out and down and saw the receding tarmac. The plane had soared into the air. All one could see was a patchwork of different colours well defined from one's viewpoint. Even then the panorama of the colours of the fields and outlines of roads was lost as the plane started to climb higher and higher into the ice blue of the sky. The fluffiness of the clouds cushioned the weight as it sped to its destination. Liz had time to look around her. Some passengers were businessmen. They had their laptops in front of them and their fingers were never still for one moment. Even up in the skies Liz thought, business as usual.

Touching down and coming to a stop, she gathered her small bag and waited, to slowly go through customs. At last she came out of the airport and got a taxi to her hotel after retrieving her case from the carousel. The hotel was a brand new tower block in the main street. It had telltale signs of just being finished, by the attendants sweeping up around and about the entrance. The large skip was in evidence where two workmen were lifting and discarding broken marble flooring that had come to grief during the process of cementing and tiling the large expanse of the foyer. Liz's hotel room was cool in contrast with the street outside. The two large windows were shuttered for the day, being thrown open as darkness fell in the evening.

Descending the stairs next morning Liz noticed several of her companions who were on the plane on the journey from England. She raised her hand in recognition then continued on to the dining room where she had a leisurely continental breakfast with the daily paper tucked under her arm. It was yesterday's paper that had been discarded. Not knowing the Italian language too well she searched the paper for a timetable. The timetable had a variety of day tours that she quickly noted. She would find the station and do some booking. For such a small place, all nationalities were to be seen.

The hotel where Liz was staying seemed to be the largest and the only one in this area. True she had seen Germans and the fair handsome Danes having breakfast in the hotel where she was staying but she realised, some of the crowds were made up of passing tourists. They were taking advantage of the beautiful coastline of the Adriatic, the sparkling azure of the sea and the sandy beaches.

Liz wandered up and down the main street noticing the odd secluded house with the tall burst of trees and nestling shrubs. The souvenir shops and the warm smells wafting in the air from the bakers shop, all inviting the holidaymaker to pause and buy. Turning down an alleyway, the hustle and bustle of the main street was muffled. The alleyway stretched in front of Liz. Cottages on both sides, some had their doors open, others closed tight to shield off the powerful sun. Some had bright looking facades others a muted wash but all giving a solid looking frontage. The roadway was partially cobbled giving way to sand and the odd tufts of long grasses. Liz walked leisurely, passing one old man, his hands gnarled with age sitting outside his cottage on a kitchen chair, his face and head covered with a shabby straw hat. On the other side, children played a type of hopscotch, their little voices full of merriment. Further down approaching the quay, an old lady was sitting by her door mending a basket. It came as a shock to Liz that the elderly ladies wore black. The lady did not raise her head as Liz past, she was too intent with the task in hand. Glistening white washing had to be ducked before Liz came out on the wharf. Here under Liz's feet, sleepers were held together by stout bolts. From the quietness of the alley the scene changed to a hive of activity. Fishermen in bright coloured vests, some without, their bronzed bodies dazzling in the sun, chattered amongst themselves, straightening and mending their nets with bill hooks. Another large net was being rolled out along the wharf. Liz stood and watched a while then retraced her steps.

Coming back into the main thoroughfare, a coach party, at least she thought it was, was hurrying down the wide street. Liz joined it hoping that it may take her to the bus station where she intended catching a bus to explore more of the district. Although alone with no companion, her anticipation and eagerness grew as she jumped on a coach. It was soon to move off and she was lucky as it was a touring coach taking in interesting towns and wayside villages and it provided a guide. That in itself was a bonus. She could not believe her luck. The coach seemed to be full to capacity as Liz strained her eyes looking for a seat. Half way down the aisle a head shot up from a seat. It was a tall man Liz noticed, half bent to allow his big frame to emerge. He motioned to her and he moved aside to let Liz slip in beside the window.

'I must not take your seat,' said Liz. She paused but he smiled and said,

'Please do, I come here most of the year and I know this area.'

Liz dropped into the window seat and then he lowered himself next to her, one leg she observed stretched out in the aisle. Being on a coach one had the advantage of seeing more. When passing through little villages children waved to them. It must be a holy day, Liz thought because surely they should have been at school. Looking through a brochure Liz discovered, with the help of the occupant next to her, the city that they were going to visit was Ravenna. She was awe struck at the tall majestic buildings as they entered the outskirts.

Stepping down from the coach her companion on the coach proffered his hand as she nearly missed her footing. They followed the guide and he paused at the monument to the dead of the Wars of Independence and Basilica of S. Giovanni Evangelista, with its bell tower reaching to the sky. On the journey Liz chatted easily to her new found friend. Nigel, was as English as they come. One would not have guessed that he was a regular holidaymaker because of his attire. He wore a shirt and tie, and a lightweight suit. He carried the jacket over his arm as they walked. Liz smiled to herself as she noticed he wore laced up shoes.

'You say you come here most of the year. How come?' said Liz.

'As I am having my car serviced this week I am taking time out visiting places I remember when I was a school boy. I am looking to see if there are any changes in the big cities, maybe new hotels which would spoil some of them.' he answered.

'Well are there?' said Liz glancing at him enquiringly.

'No! surprisingly not. The difference I find, when moving out of the ancient cities and towns, is the renovations taking place of the broken down dwellings. I am glad to see them being restored.'

The sun was beating down on them when they reached the centre of the city. They headed for a table under a bright awning and sat sipping cool drinks. Their guide pointed out to them the buildings that were of note. All of them around the square were impressive to Liz and she was glad to have bought a brochure at the outset. It was difficult to take in everything but with the brochure it would jog her memory when she arrived home. The day was spent feasting their eyes on the interiors of numerous Basilicas and the beautiful mosaics of Galla Placidia. The Good Shepherd it was soft and subdued and others, rich and vibrant in colour.

Hours flew by and night seemed to come quickly. Armed with postcards and a small sculptured plaque of the Virgin Mary, Liz and Nigel made their way back along the square. Liz looked up at the sky, it was dark and leaden and turning to Nigel, her words were whipped away from her by an almighty bang. She jumped and grabbed Nigel's arm. Thunder crashed down on them. Lightening rent the air colouring the square an electric blue. The anger of the thunder shuddered across the city. Big spots of rain gathered momentum until thrashing down it splashed their faces. Sheeting and running in rivulets, its great pace was forming whirlpools in the channels beside the pavements. It seemed bent on getting down the drains but being hindered, getting nowhere fast. The storm was interminable but suddenly the deluge slackened then stopped. The sun miraculously appeared and with a fierce heat dried up the square and dripping awnings. Soon the city started to move again, brisk business being done at the stalls as Nigel and Liz passed. The smell of new baked delicacies lingered in their nostrils as they hurried to the coach.

Handing her possessions to her as they drew up at the bus station, Nigel wondered if Liz would like to go and spend the following day with him. He voiced this to Liz. She was taken aback.

'Are you sure? I don't want to be in the way. I mean, can you be bothered to spend time showing me the sights?'

'Of course I can. I told you this morning I am taking time out. I shall have the car by tomorrow and we will drop in and see my aunt.'

'You have an aunt who lives here. That is handy. Do you make your base with her when you are over here?' Liz asked.

'No, my work is in Florence but I do try and see her often.'

He walked with Liz to her hotel. On the way they arranged to meet at ten the next day. Although tired, Liz dwelt on her day with Nigel and briefly on the outing planned for tomorrow. A feeling of excitement gripped her as she got in between cool sheets and switched off the light. How lucky she thought, to have found him and to know he did not mind showing her around the sights and to be truthful, she wouldn't have had such an enjoyable day.

Liz sat down on one of the nearby seats waiting for Nigel. Last night before arriving at the hotel, they had walked along the water's edge. The beach had been almost deserted but for a few shadowy figures. One could hear from a distance music coming from the one and only night club. Liz had been handed a flyer as she was hurrying along to the bus terminal that morning advertising an event taking place there. As they had leisurely strolled, bursts of laughter and chatter had carried through the soft night air. Waiting for Nigel it gave Liz the opportunity to jot down in her diary points that she had never realised. The ladies wearing black at a certain age. This was more pronounced in the country districts. The tumble down cottages and farm houses having been vacated and left to decay and rot, their passed occupants either dead or gone nearer the big cities to find more lucrative work.

Nigel drew up at the foot of the hotel steps. Liz noted the beautiful polished black two-seater coupé, the dashboard gleaming. Turning the ignition key the car sprang into life under Nigel's deft hands, gathering speed as he neared the outskirts of the town. It was visible they were climbing. The higher they went, the narrower the road became. The scenery took Liz's breath away. She let out a sigh.

'Oh Nigel, what a panoramic view.'

He smiled at her, not giving a comment. She was too overawed with the view. Anything that he could have said would have been lost on deaf ears.

'We are nearly at my aunt's house.' he said loudly. This brought Liz down to earth.

She turned towards him, her eyes still misty from the overpowering feeling of smallness when she had looked at the vastness. The trees dwarfing the two-seater and its occupants lined the roads on which they travelled. Occasionally a break in the trees revealed a large area with a wrought iron gate set back and through it a wide drive. Liz had noticed two of these as they passed and snaked up the steep incline. Turning left or right, inevitably Liz found the tower of a mansion partially hidden from view.

The car drew up at a lodge, the entrance to a large hotel that was glimpsed through the trees. Nigel's aunt, as Liz immediately found lived in the lodge. She was coming out of her small doorway to greet them. She had lived alone for eight years and was a comfortable lady, ample in proportions and she walked with a stick. She had a jolly face and changed her stick to her left hand to greet Liz.

'Hello my dear and you are Liz. How good to see someone from England. It is so long since I made the journey back home but when you have a stupid knee like mine, you think twice before setting off on a long journey. I am blessed with a nephew though.'

She altered her gaze and looked at Nigel fondly then turned to Liz again.

'He drives up here at every opportunity and keeps me well versed in what is happening with my children and other nieces and nephews over there. Now then, come in, I should think you will be ready for some refreshment.'

As Liz entered the low slung cottage, her eyes were riveted to a large oil painting on the opposite wall. A handsome man with piercing blue eyes looked back at them, a hint of a smile lighting up his countenance. His arresting good looks encompassed the whole room. The portrait, if taken down Liz thought would leave a void that could never be replaced, although it dwarfed the wall. Nigel's Aunt saw Liz looking at the portrait.

'That is my husband. It helped greatly to keep me going after his death. When I felt down and depressed, I only had to look at him there. He seemed to give me strength to carry on. The portrait is the only material thing I have of my past life.'

In the late afternoon Nigel and Liz walked at the back of the lodge and skirted the hotel. They came to a vantage point where they could see the winding road they had travelled. Halfway they stopped and looked at the view. Villas, sheltered and sleepy nestled into the hillsides. Others looked precarious jutting out as if with no foundation to the unaccustomed eye, but they were as steady as a rock. The road they had come along earlier was suddenly cut down to size. The muffled drone of the traffic bending, rising, snaking up the hillside was lost to nothingness.

Driving back that night after bidding farewell to Nigel's aunt, Liz said,

'How lovely the day has been. Your aunt did make me so welcome and I cannot thank you enough. If I had not met you when I did I would not have had any insight of the Italian people.'

Liz was aware, when he dropped her off at the hotel that they would say a final good bye.

'If you are ever back in Italy, do get in touch.' He handed her his card.

It crossed Liz's mind that Nigel's aunt had said the same thing. How hospitable. She knew though this holiday was a one off. She was going back as a single woman and she knew everything would be different. Loneliness would creep upon her unexpectedly more times that she would care. She shook herself, it must never happen she scolded.

Liz noticed she had jotted down that in the afternoon Harry and his cousin were coming to walk in the grounds and see the house. She had completely forgotten about them coming. It flitted across her mind if she did see them, which was most likely, she would not mention the gossip she had overheard at the post office. That would come later when Harry was down on business.

Her morning was taken up by making a good curry for herself. Liz had looked in the mirror more than once these last few days and really a good substantial meal would not go amiss. She rectified this by going to the gardener and coming back with green and red peppers, onions, cabbage and potatoes. She stuffed as much of the produce as she could manage into the dew bin, finding she had brought back far too much. The truth was the gardener had been too generous. He had piled her basket to overflowing saying as he did so that she needed fattening up. As she closed the fridge door Liz could not help but smile at his words and she had noticed the odd dress did hang on her. In the past months Liz had been snacking and not sitting down to a wholesome meal, not even when she had the time.

Harry and his cousin arrived well into the afternoon. Liz saw them approaching her. They had disentangled themselves from a group mounting the steps into the great hall. The cousin towered over her as Harry introduced him. With his height he had a big frame and instead of a casual shirt and lightweight jacket he was wearing tweeds and she noticed brown brogues highly polished. When he spoke Liz knew straight away that he was from across the border. Although a Scot, born and bred, he had lived and worked in the North of England. He was a practising vet.

'I have always wanted to come here.' Mac said.

Mac was short for Macdonald. He had been at an Agricultural Show in the borders and had met Lady Innes. She was judging the light legged horses.

'Harry tells me she died and The Racing Stables she had were sold.' Mac looked at Liz enquiringly.

'Yes that is right, and I'm in touch with the new owners Edward and Denise frequently. Edward was the trainer there when they took the stables over. Only yesterday they took me racing. I did enjoy seeing what went on. It was the first time I had been to a proper meeting and you can't really compare it with the races on the television.' ended Liz.

They paused a while looking over at the parkland in the distance then they walked slowly up the broad steps to the entrance. The rain the night before had washed and brushed the countryside clean and the sun seemed to pick out the odd places that seemed never to have been noticed before.

'Well how do you like Innes Hall as much as you have seen of it so far?' asked Liz.

'Lady Innes did say something about her home when we were waiting to inspect the show horses that time I met her but I could never have imagined anything like this.' said Mac.

'No, it is outstanding compared with some houses in the district. I am lucky to be here in such beautiful surroundings.' said Liz. She then continued.

'I was amazed at the windows when I first came here. The number of them and how tall they were. Now living here one never realises the largeness of them, only though when you are taking the curtains down or putting them up, I have to draft in a strong man even to unhook one pair of curtains.' Liz ended with a laugh.

Liz left Harry and his cousin to enjoy the interior of the Hall and some of the treasures that it housed. Before saying good-bye Harry said he would be back to see her to sort out a small matter and would Friday be convenient. Of course it was, but it left Liz wondering and worrying what the small matter was that he had to discuss with her. Liz thought more than once, could he have heard the rumour she had heard at the post office.

Chapter 10

Harry bounded up the stairs two at a time and along the short lobby.

'Mac did like this place Liz, and in fact I liked leisurely walking around, taking my time. Mac was taken with the white marble fireplace in the drawing room. It is so impressive.' said Harry.

'I am glad. Did he sign the visitors' book? Maybe he did not see it?' Liz asked

'Mac did, but he nearly didn't sign it. We came across it tucked away at the far side of the great hall leading to another entrance.' said Harry.

'Ah! that is because the visitors usually use the big entrance at first and go out by that door. If they are being taken round by one of the guides, he or she shows the party where the book is.' said Liz.

They sat drinking their coffee and Liz remembered something.

'Oh! I know what I was going to say to you, it has just come into my mind. I have always thought that John would have stuck out for half of the house.' She paused looking at Harry hoping for an answer.

'Why? It was as much yours as his and anyway I never heard it mentioned. Oh no! It is yours by right and he never raised the issue as far as

I can tell. Now then the little matter I am here about.' said Harry.

Liz inwardly braced herself. He was going to tell her that there was to be a change, something that would alter, something that would affect her.

'Are you happy Liz now that you are on your own? I think you are. You don't mind living here when all the visitors go and everything closes for the night and the gardeners go home? If you were worried about anything I hope you would tell me.' he said.

Harry drained his coffee and put the cup on the table looking at Liz waiting for her answer.

'Harry have you not heard the rumour? I thought that you were about to ask me and tell me that my position would be in question.' She waited now for his answer.

'What! It is the first I have heard tell of it. When did you hear this?'

He looked at her, concern in his eyes.

'A little time ago in the post office first, and I asked Denise if she had heard about the rumour. She had, but I couldn't enlighten her because I did not honestly know where I stood. I wish you could finally tell me one way or the other. Has Lady Innes nephew been in touch? Maybe he thinks a married couple would be better than a single woman.' she trailed off.

'Liz, this awful worry should never have happened to you.' said Harry horrified. 'Of course the nephew knows about the divorce and that in his eyes is unfortunate but it is a fact of life. In no way does it alter your position here.'

'Well that is a relief that I am staying put.' breathed Liz.

Harry and Liz walked down the great sweep of stairs and across the marble hall out on to the front where his car was parked. He nodded and raised his hand as he saw John and then turned to Liz and said.

'I shall be in touch.'

He got into his car and moved off down the drive.

'Everything alright?' called John.

'Everything is perfect.' called back Liz.

As she walked up the shallow steps, her receding back towards him she wondered if he, for a minute was curious to find Harry there and Harry not to have been to the office to see him as well. Liz was not going to give any satisfaction either, by blurting out to John what really was on her mind before Harry came. It would dawn on him that she wasn't moving and if they had thoughts about the possibility of moving into the Hall, that was scuppered by her saying. 'everything was perfect.' She paused in her thoughts. John could easily think to the contrary.

'Oh blow it. I am not going to worry my head anymore. I know where I stand.' she concluded.

The next day being Saturday, Liz was up early. Not only to open up the house but she had the morning spare to go and see, if by chance Mr Fraser would be sitting on the bench. He had introduced himself the second time they had bumped into one another. Somehow she still called him her stranger friend when alluding to him to the gardener who knew of him. In a round about way Liz had substituted him as a father figure when John's father went out of the picture. Mr Fraser was about the same age and one of the 'old school'.

Liz came to the bench and sat awhile. No sign of him. He must have gone back home yesterday, Liz surmised. 'Oh well,' she said to herself, 'He will be back in the spring.'

Liz was loath to move from the bench. The sun had come up and she could feel its rays through her thin cardigan. The day was set to be bright and sunny she had heard on the radio. Liz hoped it would be an Indian summer and shorten the winter before the clocks were changed. She looked once more searching to see if Mr Fraser was in the distance but the surroundings were bereft of anyone and anything. She turned and started walking back through the gardens. She had wanted to tell him and unburden herself a little more of her pent up emotions. The relief she had when Harry put her mind at ease.

In the afternoon one of the girls in the office tracked her down in the parlour off the drawing room. It was odd that she came looking for her because Liz had only left the office minutes before.

'What is it Jane?'

'You have visitors. They are out side the office.' said Jane. 'They are not with the group going around the house.'

Liz hurried down the corridor and came to the office door. The visitors had moved a little way from the office and were viewing a large tapestry. As soon as she saw them her spirit lightened and she quickened her steps.

'Hello! Hello! This is marvellous. When did you arrive?'

The aunt caught hold of her hands and kissed her, likewise the nephew.

Nigel's aunt said they had been in England a week and they were staying another ten days.

'We looked up how far Innes Hall was from where we are staying and the brochure gave us details when you were open. So here we are,' said Nigel putting a friendly arm around Liz's shoulder.

'How long have you been waiting?' asked Liz, and then she said,

'Come and have a cup of tea before I show you around. I am thrilled to see you both and especially you. You have made it at last.' Liz said looking at Nigel's Aunt.

As they were mounting the grand stairs taking it slowly for the Aunt and after skirting the great hall, Nigel turned and looked back at the marble hall. He had seen a number of great halls in Italy but this came very close to being one of the best.

'The park and the little bridge is so quaint before one gets a glimpse of the house.' the aunt was saying as they went ahead of him.

'It is so good to see you, and what a surprise.' Liz said again, her face showing how pleased she was by the tell tale colour in her cheeks.

The tour of the house started immediately outside the door into Liz's apartment. After refreshments they went along the wide corridor, glancing on each wall where portraits of some of the Innes family were hung. Liz pointed to one of Lady Innes. The aunt and Nigel were fascinated. Their comments as they went slowly down the line of portraits were followed by. 'Oh look! Is that the little bridge in the background where we have just come over?' or 'Look at the fine gold thread embroidered on that gown.'

Liz went ahead and opened the double doors to the drawing room. Opposite stood the magnificent white marble fireplace. They paused and took in the detail. It was well known to be the talking point of the visitor that came to Innes Hall and it was not lost on Liz's special visitors. They looked in awe at the white mantle above the fireplace reaching to the ceiling. The two chandeliers lit for the visitors were shining and sparkling, each of the hundreds of globules twinkled their brightness, all being reflected in the corners of the room. Liz opened another panelled door to the right of the drawing room fireplace and beckoned them to follow.

'Now this is the parlour to where the ladies who were staying at the Hall would retire after dinner, but come further into the room and turn to the door again.' she said.

They gasped, as in doing so an exact replica of the drawing room fireplace but a smaller version confronted them. Where there were two columns each side of the fireplace holding up the overhanging mantle shelf, it was the same again exactly. Climbing up the wall in marble, steps reached to a higher plane giving way to an open door through which could be seen the garden of Eden.

The aunt and Nigel were transfixed. Again they marvelled at the workmanship. The two cherubs each side of the open door, the lion and the lamb beautifully carved. They were visibly moved. To see one magnificent fireplace was simply wonderful, but to see two identical ones, not in size but in everything else was really something again. When they could speak at last, they told Liz,

'We will never forget these fireplaces. What craftsmen they must have had in those days.'

They moved slowly through the house pausing when something caught their eye. Peering nearer at the carvings on the doors and the fretwork in the music room. The panels depicted some musician playing his instrument and then across the room, a little girl holding up her first violin. One could imagine her mother sitting there listening to tentative raw notes, giving encouragement. On a low platform at one end of the music room was a grand piano. Liz told them that she had been toying with the idea of having concerts through the winter months. She had heard from sources and one of them who gave her interesting information, was the gardener.

'The gardener grew up here, just like his father before him. He remembers his father having to open up the music room for these sort of occasions after the war. He was just a lad in those days but he used to cart loads of chairs for the audience to sit on.' Liz said.

'The atmosphere would be perfect.' said Nigel's aunt. 'Not too vast, intimate and cosy and an audience who would appreciate good music.'

Nigel nodded in agreement. Then he said to Liz.

'Did he say anything about this place being used in other ways like a wing given over to recovering soldiers maybe?'

'No but at the time of the war it was mooted that it might be turned into a hospital but it never came to fruition. Come along to the library. I shall show you several documents Innes Hall received at the time.'

Liz went ahead and opened the door into the library. It was a long narrow room. Only one large oil painting graced the room. It was of Lady Innes' father. He was a countryman through and through. He had his dogs lying at his feet and he had paused looking over the parkland. The portrait was hanging over the mantle.

'Here they are Nigel.'

Liz pulled a ledger from one of the shelves and put it on the big round table. It contained papers concerning the war years and particularly the planned hospital. Nigel sat down and was immersed with the documents. The house was to be fortified, while the parkland provided excellent camouflage with the many clusters of trees. After long deliberations however, the powers that were then, decided to look elsewhere. At the time it was said by Lady Innes' father that the house he thought was too exposed. Whether saying that had anything to do with it he never got to know but they moved away finding a more suitable area where road, rail and communications would be better for them. Liz and her visitors now were on the ground floor and had entered the long dining room. This more than anywhere had to be maintained to the highest standard. The mahogany table taking up most of the floor space was within easy access to the new kitchens. They were situated behind the marble hall. The table was adorned with a wealth of silver and sparkling blue and gilt china. Instead of panelling on the walls, they were relieved by gold embossed wallpaper, with pictures around the walls, six in all of exotic fruits.

Nearing the end of the tour Liz showed them the old kitchens. Nigel's aunt was particularly interested in the utensils that the housekeeper and her retinue used in those days. Laid out at the end of the huge table with its benches was a recipe book. It must have been used often as it was well thumbed. The corners curling up and yellow with age.

Liz said good-bye at the entrance. Nigel had brought the car round and opened the door for his aunt.

'Hop in Else.' said Nigel.

The aunt took Liz's arm and kissed her on the cheek then she said.

'He refers to me by that name, why not you? I feel rather staid when I am in the company of young people like you.'

They were interrupted by the sound of a car flying up the drive, it stopped a little way from them. Liz turned and found it was Harry getting out of the car.

'Oh Harry, come and meet my friends from Italy.'

Harry came over and Liz introduced them. Then Nigel's aunt said.

'I was just about to ask Liz if she could join us some evening next week, maybe Wednesday, before we go home. Do you know The Swan in Little Oakwell. Nigel is it Little Oakwell or have I got the name wrong?' she turned to him.

'No you have the right place. It is about twenty miles from here.' said Nigel.

With weak protests from Liz, immediately Harry jumped to the fore.

'I will bring Liz along next Wednesday, it is Wednesday isn't it?' he paused looking at them. 'If you don't mind me tagging along.'

'That will be splendid. No buts Liz. I am telling her Nigel.'

Nigel looked at Liz, then smiled down at his Aunt and then back at Liz.

'That's settled then. No use arguing.'

He raised his hand to Harry and disappeared into the driver's seat while Liz was settling his Aunt into her seat and shutting the car door. Walking to the entrance, Liz was more than a little flustered at the way Harry had acted. He need not have offered. She turned to him at the door.

'It is awfully kind of you to take me.' Liz tailed off.

'Not a bit of it. It will be an honour.' he said teasingly.

If her cheeks were of a pale pink before, they were bright red by now as she walked quickly in front of him into the shadows of the stout front door. She thought she could handle any quips thrown at her but not seemingly when Harry was concerned. To try and control her feelings she said.

'Oh! did you leave something the other day? Have you?'

'No no. I did not think I would be back so soon but really I was going to ask if you would like to go to a musical evening. I have two tickets and it would be a shame to miss out.'

'But, but you are already taking me out to Little Oakwell.' she interrupted glancing up at him.

'I know, but I would like you to join me and go to this musical evening. It should be good. Songs from Gilbert and Sullivan, light opera, you know the sort.'

'Yes I do know the sort of thing and I much prefer that to the heavier kind but I can't accept another invitation from you. Really I can't. Anyway what about your.…...' she tailed off before she made herself sound foolish.

Harry looked at her for a second and caught hold of her hand and threw back his head and laughed.

'I am foot loose and fancy free. Didn't you know?' enquired Harry.

Liz looked up at him and started to laugh with him, and the tension eased.

Then Harry dropped her hand and said.

'Must go. See you on Wednesday.'

He got into his car and away he went raising his hand as he passed Liz and finally giving a blast on the horn.

Liz walked to the side door and went in that way. She didn't want to meet anyone at that precise moment. She quickened her pace up the grand staircase and ran the last few yards to the shelter of her own domain. There she found it safe to sort out the turmoil raging inside her. By the time she had shut the door and flopped down on the sofa her heart was hammering in her chest.

'What on earth is happening to me! Pull yourself together.' Liz said out loud to the vase of flowers on the side table. Liz had to admit that she was flattered that Nigel and his aunt had come to see her. So many good-byes and accepting the 'do look us up when you are in England or wherever,' are soon forgotten and addresses mislaid. Liz had spent a great holiday in Italy and Nigel had taken her all up and down and she had been happy again for the first time in a long while. She liked him so much and his aunt and it had been lovely seeing them again. But now the pounding of her heart was due to Harry. She shut her eyes and moaned. She must try and bury this emotion. She could not love him in that way even realising how dependent she was on him in other ways. How could she have got through the past twelve months without his constant support and help, but any one Liz had to admit to herself would have given that under the circumstances. Mulling over in her mind what so recently had happened Liz still could not stop thinking about what had occurred. She smiled when she thought of the moment Harry throwing back his head and giving a mischievous laugh. Lots of times she could remember incidents that included Harry, forgotten by him but stored away by her somewhere. They came vividly to her now.

Liz awoke with a start. She must have been exhausted and fallen asleep.

The room was in darkness. Only the last strands of light were filtering through the window.

'Oh gosh, too late to do anything now. I hope no one wanted me and came looking for me.' she pondered as she filled the kettle.

Chapter 11

Liz looked out on the countryside as they sped along. She had always driven herself these days but now on this occasion she sat back and enjoyed being driven. Passing through villages with old churches looming up, suddenly being lost to the eye by tall trees blotting out the view. Liz furtively looked sideways at Harry and then at his hands holding the wheel. She had never noticed how long his fingers were. Piano fingers her mother would have said. She turned back to look at the view again when Harry broke the silence.

'We are nearly there. Another straggly village and then we will soon be on the outskirts of Little Oakwell.'

Liz nodded and looked at herself in the mirror conveniently placed in the sun shield opposite her. Her hair was short verging nearly on dark brown and had a natural wave to it. No bother about having it professionally done or set each week. She had dressed carefully for the pending evening out, a simple cream silk dress with a fitting coat to match. The only other colour was a deep puce piping round the collar of both dress and coat. The coat fastened at the waist with one large puce covered button.

In the centre of the main street stood The Swan Inn. It was a sprawling low slung quaint establishment. What put it above all others, it had a thatched roof. The walls were white washed and there were rambling roses round the door. These again added to its charm. Harry parked the car to the side of the Inn and they got out and walked the short distance to the entrance. They were met by a slightly high pitched voice.

'We are here.'

They turned, Liz recognising Nigel's aunt at the far end of a long room. They wended their way through the tables where guests were sitting having drinks, Nigel at that point appearing behind them.

Chapter 12

Christmas came and went like the flurry of snow that greeted Liz on Christmas morning. By the time she turned out of the drive and headed for the stables soon after breakfast to spend the day with Edward and Denise, the snow had vanished leaving a bright sun and the fields and hedgerows sparkling. At this time of morning she loved it, more so because no one was about. The children still she imagined were round the Christmas tree and playing with their presents. The roads were bereft of people, cars and lorries. If it had been an ordinary day, life would have started much earlier.

'Bring your gum boots.' said Denise. 'We try and let as many of the young staff off as possible on Christmas Day. We manage with a skeleton staff and we roll up our sleeves and give a hand. Come right to the stables, we will be up there.'

Armed with suitable attire Liz went into the stable yard. Throwing open the car door and swinging out her legs she put on her wellington boots and an old jacket, not forgetting her gloves. She was looking forward to this part, doing something different and helping in a small way with the horses.

The dogs gave mouth and bounded up to her. The lurcher almost excited to see her but the old sheep dog took one look at her, recognised her and went back and laid down under the eaves. Liz found Denise coming out of a box wheeling a barrow. All that was needed for the Grey was his hay. Liz unhooked a bundle of it that was hanging on the loosebox door ready to be put into his manger. The Grey, to give him his official name was Grey Friar, affectionately known as Old Boy. He was running on Boxing Day and he was one of two favourites. Old Boy had been pointed out to Liz on one occasion when he nuzzled up to her giving her a playful nudge.

'I can honestly say, he has the run of the place.' said Edward joining Liz and Denise at that moment. 'I know some owners would

91

frown on the idea of letting their horse wander about but to tell you the truth we are powerless to stop him. At first it was irritating when he came to us and we found him freeing himself from his box and ambling around the yard. Now it is a matter of course.'

'Yes' said Denise 'and we have high hopes for him to-morrow. I am sure he wont let us down. It is an early start in the morning for him, he is off to Carlisle.'

'It is all go.' said Liz looking up at Edward. 'I am getting my eyes opened today. What time will you start off with him?'

'Pretty soon. I like my horses to be there well before their individual races even with Old Boy. He senses the excitement although he is so laid back.' Edward finished.

Armed with practically a whole turkey, plus a leg they waved Liz away. They had had their Christmas dinner at one o'clock due to the heavy day that was looming. When they had finished the morning's work with the horses, Denise had only the minimum to do regarding the dinner. As Liz travelled home the last of the sun was striving to keep its brilliance. Only a few walkers were still out and about but soon they would turn for home. Making her way in the car up the drive, no traces of sunlight and shade were visible on the bonnet. Liz got out of the car, the sun had vanished and in its place, a fog rising from the river and a steely coldness hung about her. She thought of the trip to Carlisle as she put her key in the side door and Edward taking Old Boy. She must keep her fingers crossed for a good outcome.

The holiday from Christmas to New Year was spent pampering herself. When it was not raining Liz put her thick coat on and pulled on wellingtons. The gardens were shrouded in mist some days. Other days a watery sun blinked out. Through the week Liz had telephoned Denise without success. She had tried the house phone and the stable phone. She had been told when she phoned the stables that they would be back at the end of the week. Before putting down the phone she asked how Old Boy had come on. The Head Lad said he had done what the Stables had hoped he would, he had won by two lengths.

The mantle over the fireplace in Liz's sitting room was decked with Christmas cards and the telephone was rarely still through out the festive season. Although alone, Liz loved the quietness of Innes Hall at these

holiday periods. She had been to the midnight service on Christmas Eve. The church had been decorated the week before with holly from the fields adjoining the church. Ivy was draped around the pillars leading to the chancel. It had been a good season for red and white berries and the variegated holly was strewn and secured on the sloping windowsills. The Vicar and his young wife were as charming as ever, the whole village falling in love with her when the vicar had brought his young bride into their midst. She was vibrant and outgoing. From the toddlers to the elderly, she had time to listen and learn from them. Strange at first for her being plucked from the heart of a big city, but as she settled down to country life the congregation loved to see her in the village or in her battered old Mini which the Vicar and she found invaluable.

Although Innes Hall was closed down for the festive season it was festooned with its fair share of holly and berries. Liz had asked one of the gardeners to erect the Nativity display and Christmas lights just inside the main entrance. It gave a feeling of warmth to the large vaulted hall but Liz was only too aware how quickly the holiday was drawing to a close. Twelfth Night was practically upon them.

Chapter 13

A feeling of excitement and resurgence gripped Liz as she ran down the wide staircase to open up and turn the massive lock on the front door. The weather had turned worse overnight. Steely frost met her with a blanket of freezing fog cloaking the gardens and the driveway but that did not dampen the way she was feeling. It was the beginning of a new year and that in itself was cause for hope and expectancy even if this morning was dull and grey.

Being in the public eye, a timetable had always to be adhered to and very rarely it was overlooked. It was governed mainly by the seasons. The staff members who worked at Innes Hall were glad to be back. They liked to get back to normality and take up where they left off before the break. The farmer next door at Home Farm had no holiday as such. It was a way of life for all farmers. They had chosen to work on the land and at Home Farm they were busy soon after Christmas with the lambing, bringing the ewes in to the warmth if they needed special attention. Liz appreciated and acknowledged the fact how lucky she was being placed in this position living in the heart of the country. At moments like this, she felt very humble when she thought of the friends she had made, in and around The Hall. It might have been very different if Lady Innes' nephew had frowned on divorce.

As Liz turned and crossed the hall making her way down the corridor to the office, she started to hum. 'Take a pair of sparkling eyes'. Harry had collected her on the evening of the musical concert and it had been a great evening with snacks thrown in. The latter was thought a good idea as the concert started at seven o'clock prompt and for some it would have been a rush getting back in to town. She thought briefly, could it be the concert and Harry that had given her the urge to look with hope to the future? Or was it always like this for her? Of course it was, but Harry did make a difference. Liz had no doubts about that. Liz saw less and less of John these days. When she did, it was in passing. She had seen him only this morning heading out with one of the estate men. They were busy visiting the farms. It was best to see to the upkeep and to be there when the farmer had the time to discuss and show him what needed attention and what should take priority. The six farms spreading over miles of acres took a bit of doing getting round them all and keeping them up to standard. Give him his due John was a stickler regarding the farm buildings and Innes Hall as a whole. Shabby workmanship was not tolerated.

It was that afternoon when Liz welcomed Edward and Denise. They had been away longer than intended up in Cumbria. Edward had met a friend who had racing stables in the Borders. He had persuaded Edward and Denise to visit them there and then. Denise had driven up in the land rover and one of the senior lads had driven down with Old Boy in the lorry. It was an opportunity like this Edward and Denise nearly always took, taking it with both hands. It was a great but hard life owning a stable but from time to time a little detour fitted the bill completely. Edward was always glad of the chance of seeing his friend's young horses. On this particular day they had gone to see land that the stables had bought the previous day. The parcel of land had a beck running through it and not too hilly, ideal for mares and young horses before they started training. The land joined the area that the stables occupied and the beck divided the two properties.

'How fortunate you have been, I bet you would never think that bit of land would be for sale John.' Edward had said.

'Too true. It has given the property more land and now it is in a ring fence bounded partly by a good road. I think that is the finish of me buying more land. Who ever buys this,' he had spread out his hands, 'he will have to do it if he wants more land. I am not as young as I used to be, time marches on you know.' he had ended.

'I don't believe you will ever retire.' Edward had said to him. 'And you have a great place here.'

'Well, yes, I have.' John had replied. 'I will say I have been lucky Edward and I have had good horses sent to me. Without them,' he had paused, looking at Edward, ' where would I have been these past few years? Nowhere.'

Edward had nodded. How right John was to say that. It made him think of his own stables and to vow never to slack off even for a day. How thankful he was for good keen staff.

Meanwhile Denise had gone with John's wife, Ann, to Hawick to a weekly furniture sale. They said they would be back in the afternoon. Ann had seen a picture she had liked of seagulls. On examination she had found it was a print, the original painting was by Peter Scott. She remembered a group of girls had bought a similar picture for a girl's twenty first birthday. After that Ann had always looked out for Peter Scott's paintings.

Unfortunately she had missed this one. It had been sold.

'Never mind,' she had said to Denise, 'come and see what Hawick has to offer up the main street.'

As Edward and Denise journeyed home the following day they both agreed the Borders had a rugged charm and further into Scotland, listening to Ann and John, the beauty of the hills and lochs was unsurpassed.

Liz ran to the car as they stepped out on the gravel.

'Oh, it is good to see you. I telephoned the stables and they did say you had gone up to Scotland. Time flies though. It seems ages since then.'

'You would hear about Old Boy winning at Carlisle?' Enquired Edward inclining his head towards Liz as he got out of the driving seat.

'I heard when I phoned the stables to see if you were home again. You would be thrilled.' said Liz.

Edward had brought Denise over in his car as Denise had dropped her car at the garage for its yearly check. February for them was a dear month as both cars had to be licensed, but the big horsebox and the other vehicles at the stables were licensed in the summer. By the time they were tested and all was in order, it took a hefty chunk out of the whey bill allocation. Even Liz appreciated that fact knowing how much it took to keep the estate vehicles on the road.

Chapter 14

Looking through her diary Liz had pencilled in at the beginning of the year, items that needed attention. Little items like braid that she had bought from the local town. The shop that she patronised was the only family shop still in existence selling ribbons and braids. At the far end of the shop, it broadened out to accommodate substantial mahogany shelves where bales of choice materials were kept. Every time Liz went into the shop the display in the window caught her eye. Where the materials were kept there was always a big chair with a choice piece of material draped over it. They kept the best of materials and they would go to all lengths to satisfy the customers. Nothing was too much trouble to them. It was braid Liz wanted to go round the bottom of an upholstered fireside chair that she used in the flat. She wrote it down with a list of other things and put it in her bag. Next, Liz looked at the post that she had picked up from the office earlier that morning. Inadvertently the office had put with her mail, one addressed to ... she looked closer... the letter was addressed to Angela, and it said on the next line, 'c/o Innes Hall'. Liz said this out loud, and with more than a little exasperation.

'Will I ever get rid of that red head? She is even getting a foothold in the door, my door at that!'

Liz left the offending letter on the table and quickly got the car keys from the dresser and ran down the stairs calling in at the sewing room to tell them that she would be back shortly if nothing detained her.

The sun came out intermittently through scurrying dark clouds. Big drops of rain splashed on the windscreen as she drove along. Coming in to the town she looked from left to right at the rows of cars parked in front of the shops. She slowed down near the end as she saw a car, one from the end reversing out on to the main street. Liz slid into the now vacant space. The rain petered out and Liz left her umbrella in the car. It was too windy for it, even if it rained. A tap on the shoulder made her jump and Liz turned. Standing in front of her was Nigel. She gasped. For a second she could not say anything that made sense. Then finding her voice, 'Where have you come from? Nigel how wonderful but I don't understand. You should be in Italy.'

They both hugged each other both delighted to see one another.

'Where can we have a coffee or something?' He looked around.

'Ah there is a café over there.' he said as he put his hand under her elbow and propelled Liz through the door and to a table. He laughed as they settled in their seats overlooking the square.

'You should have seen your face. You don't know where I shall pop up next. Do you?'

'No I don't. For a moment I thought I was, well I don't know what I thought. Tell me, why are you over in England? It isn't Easter yet, is it?'

'I'm here for a conference starting tomorrow. I wanted to surprise you. I have to book in at the conference building tonight. I wish I could stay longer but,' he spread his hands in resignation. 'I have to be there by late afternoon to meet up with other colleagues who are arriving at the same time.' he explained.

Being rushed, they decided to ask for the menu. It was too far to go to Innes Hall and have something to eat there, although if the circumstances had been different and he had not been governed by the conference it would have been ideal. Waiting for their order, Liz asked how his Aunt was and had he been able to get to see her.

'No, she doesn't know I'm here. I left in a hurry. The conference was put forward a week. I shall be going up there when I get back.'

They were silent for a time studying the menu then he asked.

'Everything alright at Innes Hall? And Harry? Have you seen him round and about?' He went on not letting her speak as he stretched out his hands and gripped hers across the table.

'You know Liz, I should have said something of my feelings, my true feelings on that last night in Italy. When my aunt and I met you at Little Oakwell, I knew all hope was lost when I saw you and Harry together.'

'Oh Nigel! I felt something towards you too. Of course I did, still do and I shall always have the memory of that night. If I had not met you that day at the beginning of my holiday and not met your Aunt, the poorer the holiday would have been and my existence.' Liz's voice faltered.

It was a poignant moment for them both as they looked at one another.

'I shall always remember especially that night Nigel. Not only with gratitude, but you gave me love and hope when things were at the crossroads for me at the time. I think, although I did not tell you outright, you sensed it, guessed it.' Liz ended in a whisper.

'I did sense something but I didn't want to believe whatever it was when we parted that night.'

She curled her fingers round his and said.

'I hope we will always remain good friends. Promise me that, Nigel?' she said urgently.

'I promise Liz.' He measured his words, slowly and quietly.

'I'll just be happy Nigel when you come one day, soon too, and tell me you have met a lovely girl. Whatever comes in the future, we must all keep in touch.'

When they said good-bye hugging each other Liz felt both Nigel and she would always be the closest of friends, and this meeting had given them both the opportunity to tell each other of their thoughts. Her life suddenly, a part of it had come to the fore, a part she had tried not to acknowledge, but it was stirring inside her gaining strength little by little. Liz appreciated this new awareness and Harry had filled this emptiness, this void. She was excited and nervous all at the same time. Her thoughts of him bubbled up when least expected, catching her unawares, and she had to hold herself tightly lest some of the staff should see and hear her sing out in happy abandonment.

which had been milked and was being driven to its pasture field, the farm being in the centre of the village having no way out but to drive the cows up to their field on the outskirts. They travelled along lonely roads on the way, acre upon acre of farmland and then suddenly they were on to a busy motorway.

Harry gathered speed. There was a companionable silence as they nosed their way up the motorway. The silence was broken.

'Do you know where we are going?' asked Harry.

'No I can't think where we are going. Tell me.' said Liz, smiling up at him. 'Tell me.'

'Blackpool. We are going to ride on the dodgems.'

'Blackpool! Dodgems! Really!' She said in amazement. 'You are pulling my leg. Really!' she repeated herself again.

'Yes, really. We are. As soon as we get there' Harry said.

He glanced and smiled at her briefly then at the road ahead. By his side he heard the now familiar laughter rising in Liz's throat and it bubbled out. She put her hands to her mouth trying to suppress and muffle it. Harry started to laugh at her predicament.

'It's alright, I don't mind. If you have never been on the dodgems, you are in for a treat.'

'But I have. But I never thought somehow, that you would have.' she finished.

'Ah now.' said Harry. 'There is a lot you don't know about me, but at the end of the day, I want you to know everything about me.'

Liz went quiet as the full extent of his words sunk in. She looked sideways at him. A magic moment was held briefly between them. His left hand left the wheel and lightly touched her knee. Then he changed gear and replaced it on the wheel and continued driving. After passing three lorries and getting back into the inside lane, Harry went on to tell Liz about when he was growing up.

'Every year the Fun Fair came to Edinburgh and I passed it when I went to school in the morning and when I went home at night. A few of us got to know one boy whose father owned the Fun Fair with his brother. When they were in Edinburgh, Jimmy came to our school, until they packed up and moved on. That was how I got to ride the dodgems. It still gives me a buzz when I hear of them in different towns at high days and holidays.'

Liz sat back and smiled at him. She surmised how he would look in those days. Probably not much different from the Harry she knew, broader and taller now of course but still enjoying the dodgems. She smiled again to herself and thought, 'Oh Harry, how lucky I am to be with you.'

They parked the car after they had gone down the golden mile and back again. Early holidaymakers who had come for the Easter break were already at the Fun Fair and milling around the sideshows. The coconut shy stall was the only visible one doing brisk business. The other stallholders were hastily getting their stalls ready for business when they saw their neighbour in full swing.

'Let's try this one Liz, for starters.' said Harry, handing over some money to the attendant.

Liz took a ball, throwing it time and time again but without any result. Harry threw and gathered umpteen trinkets on the way, finally a doll dressed as a Spanish Flamenco dancer with shiny oiled hair, at least the appearance of oiled hair. Long dangling earrings and a beautiful tiered frilly dress.

'Here you are,' he said as he handed the trinkets and the doll over.

'Isn't she gorgeous!' Liz exclaimed.

'Come on, we are going to find the dodgems. Can you hear the rumblings of a generator starting up, I can?' asked Harry.

Liz followed, passing the merry- go- rounds with the little horses, the children climbing on to them ready to enjoy the ups and downs of the bobbing horses as it started to move. Their little faces were a treat to see.

Massive machines towered above them. The waltzers were not yet spinning on their undulating track as the man in charge was oiling the mechanism of the engine before starting it up. Harry had nearly given up hope of ever finding the dodgems when, suddenly, going through the passage at the left hand side of the waltzers they came to them. Already a row of hopefuls rushing towards it, other holiday makers climbing the three steps at intervals handing their money to the man in charge. The music struck up and Harry steered Liz towards a gaily-painted red dodgem. They quickly settled into it and before they had time to look around themselves the rumbling of the engine and the music got louder and in seconds they were careering around trying not to bump into the other dodgems coming towards them. They rattled around only to find themselves being shunted from the back and bumped at both sides. Extricating themselves from the tangled heap, they found themselves in the same predicament in the next turn of the wheel. Laughter rang out from both sides. At last the dodgems slowed down coming to a stop. Harry eased himself out of the seat holding out his hand to Liz, as they negotiated the steps and got on to the ground. No sooner they were on terra firma they were whizzing through the air on the waltzer, swooping and diving one minute, the next, trying to cling to their seats, ever fearful of being yanked out of them, only then the laws of gravity coming to their aid.

Liz jumped down into Harry's arms as the waltzer came to a halt.

'Harry.' she laughed. 'Isn't this great. It is years since I have enjoyed myself like this.'

Harry let go of her but kept hold of her hand.

'Are you game for just one more?' He paused then said. 'The Roller Coaster.'

He paused again then still holding her hand they dashed to where the Roller Coaster was and joined the end of the queue. Clamping themselves in they waited for the now familiar rumble of the switchback. Slowly it gathered momentum, rising higher. The music blared and Liz now was holding her breath. The occupants tied in seemed to be hovering up in the sky. Suddenly with a swish they were hurtling down, the ground fast coming to meet them. No sooner they had seemed to touch the ground, they were hauled up into the sky again. Screams were heard from the front and the back of them and Liz added to their volume. Harry covered one of her hands reassuringly laughing at her. Up and down they went until they could feel the movement of the coaster gradually change gear and eventually trundle to a stop.

Liz fell against Harry as she stepped on to the ground. She smiled up at him.

'I am quite dizzy but I wouldn't have missed that for anything.'

'Come on I am famished. Let us find somewhere, where we can have a good meal.' Harry said.

'I am a little peckish too. Gosh, is that the time! We had better hurry else we wont get in anywhere.' she said.

Ensconced at a table for two which the occupants had just vacated they settled down and studied the menu. The waitress came and went after getting their order. Liz looked around and then at Harry.

'Weren't we lucky to get this table. Look, they are turning people away.'

Their order came after a time and they tucked in to it.

'I was ready for that,' said Harry putting his knife and fork down on the plate. 'I must have been hungry.'

'And the sea air would help.' smiled Liz.

They finished their coffee and Harry went to pay the bill while Liz went to freshen up. She found him waiting for her on the pavement. They negotiated the wide street with its trams and horse drawn vehicles and milling people before they stepped on to grass and sand at the opposite side away from the hubbub of the fair and its jollification. The sea threw up its seaweed smell. A sign her father used to say brought on a change in the weather Liz told Harry. Liz had told Harry that her father and mother were both dead. At the time Liz could not speak about them in case she broke down. It was a dreadful period as they died within a month of each other. Now the months had grown into years and Liz could talk of them.

They wandered on. Occasionally Harry and Liz would pick up a piece of stick or driftwood and throw it as far as they could. She still carried the

Spanish doll and she was thankful that she had a generous shoulder bag to store it away along with the added trinkets that Harry had won for her. What a day to remember. She voiced this to Harry and Harry took her into his arms.

'We are going to have many more days like this Liz, I promise you,' and he bent his head to her upturned face.

With their arms around each other they turned and slowly walked back the way they had come.

That night after Harry had dropped her at the side entrance and had seen she was safely ensconced in the hall, Liz mulled over the day's happenings. She wanted to dwell on every moment of the day she had spent with him. She held herself tightly, a little scared of the feelings that were welling up inside her. Ecstatic one minute, the next full of doubt as to whether she had taken his words too seriously. Her feelings might just explode and shatter into a thousand pieces.

Liz was jerked out of her reverie by the persistent ringing of the telephone. She struggled out of her preoccupied state and lifted the receiver. It was Harry.

'Liz, I'm in the office getting some papers together. I have to be in London tomorrow. I cannot tell you when I shall be back.' His tone was business like as if he was talking to his secretary. Liz's heart plummeted to the ground. The only thing she could voice was a strangled 'Oh.'

There was a long pause at the other end of the phone then he said urgently,

'Liz, Liz. I love you.' and he rang off.

She stood transfixed. All the little doubts were suddenly without foundation. She stumbled on to the sofa, thinking a moment ago her day with Harry meant nothing to him but now it meant everything when she had heard his last words.

Chapter 15

No one had missed her yesterday, at least no one said anything. Liz was glad of that but she had her suspicions. Liz had seen two of her helpers at the far end of the corridor. They were bound to have seen her when she had run down to meet Harry waiting for her, and then she was never seen right through the day. The feeling Liz had since last night stayed with her, it was so overwhelming. What have I done to deserve this lovely man? Her mind lost in thought, she headed away from the building. It took all her time to focus on the matter in hand. This was a letter sent to her from the Charity that she and John had hosted last year. It seemed to Liz, longer than only one year. With the charity behind them that was nothing compared with the rest of the year that followed. Finally for her with all the unseen worries and the divorce and the niggling annoyances caused by the red head, it ended up happily.

Liz saw the Head gardener going into one of the glasshouses. She followed him in and up the middle aisle flanked by the benches that housed the hundreds of seedlings ready to be re-planted into bigger pots.

'I am glad I have caught you.' Liz said, 'I have had a letter from the Charity we supported last year. Do you think you could forward some pot plants and produce for sale for it this time?'

'When do you say it is? The first Saturday in July?'

Liz glanced at the letter.

'Yes that is the date.'

Liz left the gardener and went to the various departments concerning the help wanted when the charity took place. If all the helpers were free and would give a hand, Liz could tick that off the list. Everybody said they would help and some of the old stagers voiced it was like old times. They had thought this last year. Liz was pleased that they felt that way. It cemented a day in the calendar that had been missing since Lady Innes had died.

After writing to the president of the charity Liz got the folder to check everything was tabulated and from that, she found the telephone numbers of the various people they used last year. It was lucky she had the foresight keeping everything intact. It would have been more work if she had done away with the details. After the confirmation of the event, Liz would be ready to set the wheels in motion and hopefully everything would go to plan. As for John, he had seen Liz and had heard of the charity being held there again. He would lend his hand, in any capacity if Liz needed him on the day. That she thought cleared the awkwardness between them. Last year he had been very much in the front line.

The week seemed to hurry by. The weather was fresh and the young leaves were showing themselves in the trees. The bread and cheese in the hedgerows was barely out but the May blossom in the fields was showing off its beautiful displays. Spring was a sparkling fresh season to start off the year Liz always thought.

One night Liz was rummaging around looking for her old diary. The truth was she had not heard from Harry since he had gone up to London and she was trying to make herself busy. It was over a week and writing her innermost thoughts in her diary would help, if it were possible, and to lighten the ache whenever she thought of him. Liz found the diary at the back of her dressing table drawer. She opened it and was oblivious of the -time as she covered the pages. From the beginning, to the moment she put down her pen, she had written in detail everything that had happened to her. She was so alive to her feelings for him that she could hardly contain herself. Thinking of him these last few days made life easier at first but following those thoughts were the little doubts that reared up trying to stifle her, these were so unbearable. Oh gosh please, please let me hear from him soon. Liz brought the green silk ribbon marker neatly down the page and shut the diary, putting it safely at the back of the drawer where she found it. She was aghast when she looked at the time. Ten to ten. Liz folded up and went to bed.

Liz put plans straight into operation as she had word from the Charity's President. Her reply had come by return of post and she, the President, was ever so grateful to Liz taking the bulk of the organising on her shoulders. It meant the office was involved and every area of Innes Hall leant its support. The different departments got on with their particular input until they all came together. Not until they were satisfied would they sit back and wait for the big day. Liz went up to her flat and read the details of the luncheon once more. At this stage it was vital that she missed nothing out. It was now she could telephone the caterers. Looking at the menu of last year, Liz thought a few people that were at the function a year ago might easily turn up again. Minor adjustments would have to be made, meaning slight ones.

'Hello! Hello there!' The sound was coming from the wide landing at the top of the grand staircase. It was Harry's voice.

'Harry!' Liz blurted out, her voice breaking into a sob. She jumped up from the kitchen table opened the door and flew down the short corridor, slipping and skidding to a wobbly halt against him and finally the humiliation of falling at his feet. She looked up at him, her face bright crimson, agitation rising in her. Harry bent down and grasped her hands and lifted her up beside him, not missing the one solitary tear running down her cheek.

'Liz, what is the matter?' he asked, gathering her close and bending his head to wipe away the tear.

'I thought you weren't coming back. I know it is silly of me but you seemed to have been away such a long time.' she finished in a small voice, hardly a whisper

'Never think that, Liz. You have got me for good.' and he pressed his face against her hot cheek holding her tightly.

Liz took Harry the short distance back to the flat and switched on the kettle and brought two beakers out of the cupboard.

'Has much been going on? Have you been busy?' Harry asked as he sat down. 'I see the visitors are enjoying the gardens.' Looking out, even now at the beginning of the season there was a steady stream making their way to the gardens.

'No not really. We have the day to day running well taped, I think. Look,' and she glanced at the sofa. 'The letter came from the charity John and I hosted last year, that is the most pressing at the moment.' she finished.

'Are you going to do it then? It will be a lot of hard work initially.'

'Yes, but luckily I have spoken to all who helped last year and some of the helpers are eager to start preparations right now, but the best of it, I have kept details from last year, so it will be a lot easier in that respect.'

The conversation turned to Harry's time in London. He told Liz a little of what he had been doing whilst away and then they gave themselves the pleasurable time, of simply being together in one another's company.

When Harry had gone, it was hard to settle to anything right away. Liz rang Denise on the off chance of finding her in. No luck, but instead of getting in touch with the caterers, she took her jacket off the hook on the back door and went down the wide expanse of the avenue, through the wicket and into the parkland. Liz saw him taking his seat on the bench. He had his back to her. She quickened her pace and nearing him she shouted.

'Mr Frazer Mr. Fraser.' and she started to run the last few yards to him.

'Oh Mr Frazer! how good it is to see you. I have been to the bench so many times I've lost count. At last you are here.'

'What a welcome! But tell me about you. You look a different girl. You looked as if you had the cares of the world on your shoulders when I saw you last. What a transformation.' said Mr Frazer.

'You could say a lot has happened since I saw you last but did you go abroad to sunnier places last year?' Liz asked.

'No I stayed at home and round and about. I had to, as we had a festival in our village. We all did our bit to make it successful.' he replied 'Tell me.' said Liz. 'How long did it go on for? A weekend?'

'No, it went on for a week. It opened with a service on the Sunday, and finished with a service on the following Sunday.' said Mr Frazer.

'A week!' Liz exclaimed. 'That would take a great deal of organisation.'

'Well it did, but we do have events frequently. Granted this was the biggest last year. We have to think of the upkeep of our beautiful church. It needs constant looking after especially the heating system and then our thriving school,' Mr Frazer paused, ' but it was the cathedral in the city six miles away, that we voted to have the bulk of the money given over to. Musical evenings, garden fetes, that sort of thing we had. Every day or evening was taken up with something, culminating with a service ending the week's activities.'

'Gosh you have had your hands full.' Liz said.

They chatted some more and then Liz remembered at the back of her mind the picture hanging up on one of the walls, which she wanted to mention to Mr Frazer.

'I wonder if you have time to come up to the house? I would like to show you something.'

'Well, this is very mysterious.' Mr Frazer gathered up his walking stick and started walking to the house with Liz.

'I have never heard you mention ever being in the house since we moved here.' Liz enquired, looking at him?

'No, but I used to be a regular visitor some years ago. I don't imagine it is changed much, has it?' ended Mr Fraser.

'The new kitchens have been built on the ground floor and the old kitchen is part of the tour where the guides take the visitors.' said Liz.

They went into the Great Hall and across its black and white marble floor and slowly ascended the lovely staircase. Memories flooded Mr Frazer's mind. Thirty years slipped away replacing them with an era of carefree days. His time was spent at Innes Hall with an assortment of cousins. Happy days he remembered. One cousin arrived on his motorbike. Every summer it was the same, until another stage in life beckoned.

Liz and Mr Fraser reached the top of the stairs and walked along the wide space of the landing. He looked from left to right at the landscape paintings and came to an abrupt stop at the portrait that Liz was going to mention to him.

'Good gracious, he is still hanging here.'

'That's the mystery,' said Liz. Don't you think he looks like you?'

Mr Frazer roared with laughter. He could not stop.

'Oh my goodness! Do you think so? I cannot see any resemblance.'

'Why do you say that? I think he has something that resembles you?'

Liz stood back from the portrait and considered it again. 'May be not.'

Mr Frazer went on to tell Liz that he had been a friend of a cousin who used to be here in the summer holidays.

'We used to get up to all sorts of things, fishing in the river, climbing trees. We built a tree house once in a great big oak in the park. The tree is still standing but I doubt the tree house will not be there now.'

'What a great time you must have had, I am quite envious.' said Liz.

'But getting back to this picture.' continued Mr Frazer. 'When it rained, we came into the house and sat under this picture and made this man our hero. We consulted him on everything we did. We planned our day under his presence. Looking back to those days, we must have been mad. Peering closer and bending to the left hand side of the frame he said to Liz.

'Look! I've found it.'

Liz looked where he indicated. Scratched on the frame were their initials.

C.I. and R.F. Cameron Innes and Robert Frazer.

'Are you still in touch with him?' She enquired.

'It wasn't many years before Cameron went off to Africa. We kept in touch off and on. We were both trying to make headway in our chosen careers. He went out to one of the schools there at first, but soon he moved up country.' said Mr Frazer.

'Did you keep in touch though?'

'Oh yes but unfortunately, he came down with some sort of fever and he died suddenly.'

'Mr Frazer, how dreadful! How sad! One of your best friends.' Liz said feelingly 'Yes he was, but it was a long time ago. I still kept in touch with Lady Innes you know. She and I spent hours sitting on the bench in the summer and she always tagged on when we built the tree house. She was handy when we wanted someone to hold a hammer or a suitable piece of wood.'

They were silent for a while then Liz said.

'You have heard me mention Denise and her husband Edward. They told me about Lady Innes' accident but she did get back to getting around again, even though she relied on a stick.'

'She did indeed. I think everyone who knew her was shocked when they heard of her death. Being here all the time, she grew up with everyone.

Innes Hall as you know, employed a lot of people round and about and the same now, so she knew them right from the start.' said Mr Frazer.

'True,' said Liz, 'and we earn our daily bread.' She smiled up at him.

Next time Liz thought, she would tell Mr Frazer how happy she had become in the company of Harry. In the meantime she loved the time when work had finished. With Harry not there, her thoughts were never far from him. How could she be as happy. Never did she think she would meet a kind generous man like Harry and then find herself falling in love with him and he loving her in return.

Chapter 16

The day was fast approaching for the charity function. The chairs and tables arrived the previous day and willing helpers had carried them in and set them up in the great hall. The table linen and gleaming cutlery, which had come the day before was now on the tables, and the cutlery was glinting where the shafts of light flooded through the windows. The big urns of flowers were in place in the hall and to welcome the guests at the entrance, members of the staff would be there to usher the guests to their tables.

The President and her retinue arrived on the said day and were in evidence at the top table. As soon as the guests were assembled the President welcomed them all and said a few words about the charity and added that she hoped they would enjoy the luncheon and to give as generously as they could to help the cause.

The storm erupted the following Monday. It came without a sign. Not the thunder and lightening sort but the storm between John and the red head. Liz heard more than raised voices. Their shouting match reached crescendo pitch. She ran along the corridor to the top of the staircase and although they could not be seen, their loud angry voices were coming from the hall.

At the height of their shouting, Liz had got to the curve of the stairs and John saw her. If it were possible to explode more John did, and he roughly steered the red head to the side door saying.

'Don't be so stupid, you can not go to her flat.'

Before the side door banged shut behind the two of them, Liz heard clearly.

'Why not? I have a right to be here.'

Liz walked down the remaining steps and into the hall. Not only had she witnessed the fracas but the office staff and the postman also. Liz could imagine the tongues wagging and knowing the postman, he would have a field day recounting the morning's happenings at Innes Hall. Liz pondered on some of the ladies hearing with their own ears what had gone on this morning. They would be shocked and stunned. Innes Hall had never experienced that kind of behaviour before. Liz too was aware that the same helpers would think the episode this morning would not have taken place if Lady Innes had still been here. Liz thought she should tread carefully. She did not open up the conversation to any of the staff members when she was with them throughout the day. The sooner it was forgotten, the better. It should not have happened. What on earth was John thinking about to bring her in earshot of the staff. It was disturbing too for Liz to hear the redhead's intention of coming up to the flat. But thank goodness she was waylaid. The audacity of the girl!

No sooner had she thought of this Liz was confronted by her. Her red hair although framing a face that Liz imagined would be pretty, now held hatred in its blue eyes. Liz was horrified. It was half past five and the helpers were going home. Liz was taken off her guard. If she did not think otherwise, she could have thought the redhead could have gained the landing where Liz was, by sneaking up the back stairs. Liz gathered herself and faced her.

'Oh! 'Are you lost? You are on the right road now. Down the stairs, across the hall and you can not miss the front door.' Said Liz.

Immediately Liz turned and headed for the safe confines of the flat, thinking all the time why should the redhead be a threat to her. Liz did not look back. She half expected an outburst or worse, feet following her into the flat. Nothing like that happened. Could it be that the redhead was insecure and really not sure of herself. Liz stopped going down that avenue and quickly said to herself, 'who is kidding whom, she knows what she is doing, for that is a fact.'

Innes Hall settled down to an organised, well run establishment as before. There were no repetitions of the redhead's outbursts, John had seen to that. He never said anything to Liz either, although Liz knew full well he was aware she had seen and heard everything. Liz thought it best too to keep her own council, but it had rocked her more than she dared to admit. It was an impossible situation looking at it one way but on the other, a little voice said to her, 'rise above it.'

This was all well and good, but the red head wanted to boot her out by any means possible and get herself ensconced at Innes Hall.

It was the next day Liz saw Denise down at the village.

'I was coming on spec to see you.' said Denise.

Liz's eyes lit up. She wanted some female company right now to unload her troubled thoughts to, someone like Denise, especially Denise. Liz told her to go up to Innes Hall and she would catch up with her.

They settled around the kitchen table with their mugs of coffee.

'Edward wanted me to go with him up to London. He was doing business and popping into the Jockey Club. It was a short stay but I did feel that I was letting you down. It was the time when you were busy having the charity as you know,' said Denise.

'Oh don't bother about that,' said Liz. 'It went well, like last year. We made a good sum of money, even if we did not have a celebrity to open the proceedings.'

'Who did it? Anyone or no one?' Denise enquired.

'Oh the Lady president did it. She just said a few words prior to sitting down to lunch. More coffee?'

Denise handed her mug and Liz filled it up.

'But you will never guess what happened yesterday, it took place in the great hall—a real ding-dong of a row between the redhead and John. The staff heard the commotion. They came out of the various places where they were working.'

'Oh Liz, what did you do?'

'Well I was powerless to do anything and worst of all, the postman witnessed it. So you can imagine it will be all over the village by now.' Liz paused and then continued. 'I shall probably blurt out to Harry the whole episode when he comes, but most likely he will have got to know about it on the way. We are a close community so I cannot expect anything else. But I do wish it hadn't happened.'

'Don't worry, it will be soon forgotten but I can imagine how annoying it is to you.' said Denise.

Liz waved Denise out of sight and turned and went back into the great hall, up the stairs and into the flat. She made herself a light salad and ate it at the kitchen table. It was a lovely day, as was the beginning of the week and Liz wondered when the weather would break. It was too good to be true but everyone was taking it in one's stride enjoying it while it lasted.

The familiar short burst of his horn made Liz aware of Harry getting out of his car and making his way inside. Liz was at the back of the Hall and she dropped what she was doing and hastily went inside and followed Harry on to the landing. He turned as he heard light footsteps.

'I thought it would be you.' he said, as he gathered Liz in his arms and with a mischievous glint in his eyes,

'I bet you have missed me.'

As quick as a flash, Liz wriggled out of his arms laughingly saying.

'Indeed not.' and flew along the landing, gaining the door of the flat, with Harry in hot pursuit. He picked her up and with a nudge on the door with his knee he deposited her on the sofa.

Liz could not contain her giggles and she tried to jump up. Two big hands bore down on her shoulders pressing her on to the cushions. His mouth found hers. He explored the line of her cheekbone, kissing her brow then moving his mouth to the hollows of her neck. Liz was aware of his taut body against hers. In turn her body became attuned with his and now they moved as one. She gave herself completely. Harry traced her lips with a light finger. Liz was lying quiescent in his arms. She reached up and caught his hand pulling it down and held it close against her face.

'Oh Harry, darling Harry.'

She had never said to Harry, how really she felt before but this time Liz could not withhold it anymore. Harry bent his head and sought her mouth

with urgency. Again they were bound together as if they were one. Their lovemaking was harsh and sweet, one moment tender, the next without warning, fighting the desire to throw away barriers. The longing for the ultimate and eventually gaining that higher plane which he and she would reach, for now had to be put on hold.

After seeing Harry's car out of sight, being obscured by the bend after it had gone over the hump backed bridge, Liz had to shake herself as she made her way walking up the shallow steps to the stout studded door. How many times she had entered this way and paused as she looked around at the beautiful surroundings. She loved the quietness when the day's work was over and the helpers and gardeners had long gone. Innes Hall and the immediate surroundings settled down to a magical peace. Harry had commented on this fact as he slid into his car and she had agreed.

'Pity though.' he had said slowly as he drove away.

'I wonder why he said that.' she now thought.

Liz caught her breath suddenly, every nerve in her body sprang to life. Her pulses started to race. Had he been in touch with the owner? Had he told Harry that he was coming home to take up residence? Could it be, the owner was leaving America for good? Liz straight away knew her services would not be required. A terrible thought occurred to her, what if he wanted to sell it? Liz could not bear the thought of that and dismissed it quickly. 'Preposterous.' she said audibly looking around her as she was still outside. Then something came flooding back to her memory. When she and John had been seeing about Innes Hall, right at the beginning, Harry had told them that Innes Hall would never go under the hammer because of a multitude of cousins. Even so, Liz would rather like to know one way or another, then maybe she would have to put her thinking cap on. Climbing the stairs to her flat, her old home came into her mind. If the worst came to the worst Liz had that to fall back on. Liz stopped short. 'How ridiculous,' she exclaimed to her self. Harry would have told her if anything were to change but with her heightened senses Liz was alive to everything that Harry said. She put her last thoughts out of her mind. Surely, Harry would have told her even when they were so wrapped up in each other. 'Oh yes, he would.'

Before Liz fell asleep, it came to her, she had completely forgotten to tell Harry about the rumpus the day before between the redhead and John.

Chapter 17

Liz's head was buzzing with pieces of news that she wanted to tell Harry. The most recent and flabbergasting news came when Edward and Denise drove up the next day.

'Hello, lovely to see you again. Two visits in two days, one after the other.' Liz ended with a laugh.

Edward came straight to the point by saying to Liz, 'We have some news Liz. I know Denise was with you yesterday, but we did not know until late afternoon, and she could not say anything then.'

Liz looked perplexed and said. 'But what is it?'

She nearly blurted out to them about them having a baby, but she bit her lip and waited expectantly.

'We are leaving the Racing Stables, Liz.' Edward and Denise said in unison. Edward went on.

'We wanted you to know right away from us. We did not want you to hear from someone else.'

For a moment Liz was speechless then hugged them both.

'But where are you going? I hope it isn't miles away. You know you are the only friends I have apart from the friends I have in the village.'

Edward put his arm around Liz's shoulder affectionately and the three of them sat down in the flat. Liz got up and said.

'Does this call for a drink?' automatically reaching into the dresser and bringing three glasses and wine and pouring the liquid into them.

As Liz settled on the sofa again, Edward told her all about the transaction. Not only selling the racing stables, they sold the horses too, as a going concern and then they bought another property with a string of horses already there. At that point Denise jumped in.

'Guess where?' she said.

Liz could not think straight. She asked

'I can't think where. You will have to tell me. Is it further down south?'

'Do you remember Edward took Old Boy to Carlisle on Boxing Day and met an old friend who has Racing Stables over the Borders? That is where we are going.' Denise said.

'Well I go to sea.' said Liz. 'It's miles away. But, but I am happy for you, but oh dear, I'll not see you both for ages. I shall miss you so much and our tete a tetes, Denise.'

'It wont be too bad.' said Edward. 'When I went to Carlisle to the races, it did not take long and it was frightful weather. Carlisle is just this side of the Borders.'

With Edward saying that, it didn't seem too far. All the same, in a way, Liz knew she would be bereft with them going.

Later in the day Liz noticed a fair amount of visitors were being shown around. They emerged from seeing the Drawing Room and were now starting to view the pictures on the walls. Skirting the Great Hall Liz came in contact with another group nearing the end of the tour. Innes Hall was doing brisk business but she thought to herself 'I should be doing something too, the musical evening perhaps.' but it wasn't going to be voiced that day. Liz had put out feelers on that score to the people in and around Innes Hall. The older members were all for it but the seventeen and eighteen year olds were dragging their feet. They wanted to know and have a say in the matter before they would commit themselves. Liz secretly welcomed that comment. She would get in touch with the local school. Something might come out of it but she did not do anything about it there and then, Liz was still thinking of the news Edward and Denise had imparted that morning.

Some time later Harry and Liz were down by the river. They turned and walked up the incline on to the level ground and retraced their steps back to the bench. Liz had flown to him when she had first seen him, putting her arms around his neck glad to see him, he gathering her close. He had been away on business and Liz had not expected him for a few more days. It had been a busy day at Innes Hall and Harry had surprised her.

'I've got loads to tell you.' she said. 'First of all guess who is leaving? It is Edward and Denise. You know, the Racing Stables.'

'Oh yes, I know them. Where are they going?' asked Harry.

'A few miles over the Borders. I shall miss them dreadfully. Denise and I got on so well. They said they would always keep in touch. Of course they will, but it is not like living a couple of miles away, is it?' ended Liz.

'No it isn't, but you have still got me.' Harry said as he caught her hand and gave her a reassuring hug.

Liz looked up at him and smiled, then continued the saga of things that she was remembering to tell him.

'Then after the function, I was walking along the top corridor when I heard John and the red head having an almighty row in the Great Hall. Harry, at that moment I wished that you had been here. Some, well mainly all the staff came out of the different rooms where they had been working and the one man I dreaded hearing the rumpus was the postman. He was bound to tell some of the villagers.'

'Well! I thought better of John. What did you do?' asked Harry.

'I went down to the curve of the staircase and he glanced up and saw me. He hurriedly hustled her out of the side door.' said Liz.

'You must have seen him since then. What did he say to you?' Harry wanted to know.

'That is the point.' said Liz. 'I was very careful in not engaging talk with any of the staff and not with John, but my blood was at boiling point, I can tell you. The audacity of the pair, especially letting it happen at Innes Hall. Thankfully the office did not raise it either.'

'What a time you have had. I wish I had been here.' and he caught her to him.

'But wait a minute.' Liz said. 'That is not all. I found the redhead up on the landing after that.'

'What!' he was astounded. 'Up on the landing leading to your flat?'

'Yes that one' Liz paused then she said. 'I don't know how I did it, but as calm as I could, I said, oh! have you lost your way? I pointed her in the direction of the grand staircase. I fled, turning on my heels and I headed for the flat, half expecting her to come after me.'

'Oh Liz, that was awful. You haven't had any more brushes with her, have you?' Harry looked perturbed.

'No, no, of course not, but the redhead's sole mission was to accost me on my own territory and tell me to vacate Innes Hall. If you speak to the office, they will tell you. They heard as much as I heard Oh Harry I've said too much. I'm sorry but it did shake me at the time.'

'Liz how appalling for you.' said Harry. 'I will tell you what I shall do Liz. I shall find out where John is to-morrow, and go and see him. You shouldn't be put through this ordeal. It is preposterous the way this girl is going on. I wonder what she hopes to achieve.'

Liz looked at Harry enquiringly, but he did not say anything and she hurriedly said,

'Please say nothing. It would stir things up again. At least we seem to be running on an even keel once more.' Liz ended.

They moved away from the bench making their way to the avenue. Liz told Harry as they walked, of bumping in to Nigel in the market town. It was most unexpected.

'He was over for a conference, and he was making his way to Innes Hall.' said Liz. 'It was good that we met that way. If he had gone to the Hall, he would have been terribly rushed and found me not there. He had to be at the conference by six to meet up with other members.'

'How is his aunt? She seems to be on the ball with most things. She must like living up in those hills. Her coming home to England to live, she was saying has no appeal.' Harry remarked.

'Well no. I suppose putting down roots so long ago, Elsie wont want to make such a change again. Her friends and the community around her are in Italy, not in England, not anymore.' said Liz. Then Liz went on to tell him. 'It was great to see Nigel, Harry. I can't forget my time in Italy. If I had not met him, I would not have seen a quarter of the places he showed me, and I would never have met his aunt and been invited into her house.

Harry was silent as they went through the wicket into the avenue. Liz looked at him, then quickly away. Could it be a hint of rivalry in his demeanour that she saw?

'I feel a bit jealous believe it or not, you and Nigel, but remember, you are mine.' He took her hands in his and gathered her close.

She could hear her heart beating loudly. Liz hid her face against his chest. At these odd moments, it was hard to describe how truly she loved him. The feeling was too much to bear, but spoiling this lovely moment, at the back of her mind, jostling for position was the thought of the nephew returning from America and she having to relinquish the reins of Innes Hall. Liz dared not think about it anymore. She suddenly uttered it to Harry.

'Is it true?' Liz wanted to know. Lifting her eyes, searching his to see a reaction, any sign that she could find her answer.

'Darling I don't know what you are talking about. If you could give me an inkling what is going on in that pretty head of yours, I may be able to tell you if it is true or not.'

'Now I feel silly and stupid.' Liz trailed off.

'Come on, out with it.' he said, 'I don't like it when you worry.'

Liz didn't want to voice it, but she knew Harry would not rest until she said what it was that had been troubling her. Liz summoned up enough courage and haltingly told him.

'Can you remember when you were getting into your car last time? We had been talking about how peaceful it was, when the day's work was done.' Liz paused and then went on. 'You said, ' pity though.' It got me wondering. I could not ask you then because you were driving off. It was a strange thing to say.' Liz finished. She looked at him expectantly even a little nervously.

'Well, I always like it here. I only wish I could spend more time with you. But at the moment, especially at this time of year it is difficult.' Harry ended drawing her near and planting a fleeting kiss on her lips.

The clouds, not only one, lifted and she felt relief. The nephew in question receded into the background, her worries unfounded. Liz smiled up at him. How could she think otherwise. Is that what living on ones own does to one? Liz hurriedly dismissed the thought.

Harry and Liz entered Innes Hall by the side entrance and as they were mounting the stairs Liz remembered seeing Mr Frazer.

'Oh! I was meaning to tell you, I saw Mr Frazer on the bench the other week. We had a good chat. He was telling me about when he was a boy, he used to come to Innes Hall for his holidays. He was a school chum of one of the cousins who spent all his summer holidays here. I brought him up here to see this picture.' She paused. 'I thought the man in the portrait resembled him in some ways. I told him so too. Mr Fraser roared with

laughter. He did say though, the two of them hatched their plots, sitting under the picture.' Liz pointed at it as they passed.

They went in to the flat, and Liz went to close the kitchen window and the others in the sitting room. Harry caught her arm and said.

'It is early yet. We could have some supper in town and finish off going to the pictures. What about it?'

No sooner Harry suggested it, Liz grabbed her bag and they hurried down to the car. The now familiar giggle rose in Liz's throat.

'Isn't this exciting. It reminds me of sitting in the back row.' she said slipping into the seat beside him.

Most eating houses were closing down as they parked the car in the main street but there was one café near the picture house. This one stayed open to catch the picture goers and it did a roaring trade most nights in the week. Harry ushered Liz to a table in the far corner and they sat down. She looked around at the sturdy tables, three long rows with ample space between them. Each table had four table settings only their table and another one in the other corner, she noticed had place settings for two. The waiter came and went with their order. Liz smiled at Harry but did not say anything because swiftly she looked out of the window as she felt his leg touch hers and press it against hers. Harry reached out and held her hands making her turn her face and look at him. For a moment they were lost in each other's gaze until they were aware of the waiter coming towards them. The waiter put down their plates and went. Somehow Liz managed her meal but could not dismiss the incident that had occurred minutes before. She wondered if Harry had the same feeling she had when he had touched her below the table. She tried to reason with herself not to be silly, of coarse he would think nothing of it. It was just one of these little interludes but helping her with her coat as they were ready to leave, Liz sensed an awareness that had not been there when they had started out an hour ago. As they walked down the short way to the picture house he held her arm tightly and as the lights dimmed the pressure of his arm resting along her shoulders gathered her towards his warm body.

As they parted that night they had to prise themselves away. They knew they had never been so happy. Liz in a happy daze got into bed willing herself to stay awake long enough so that she could remember every thing that had made the night so special. To other people it would seem so trivial but to Harry and her it meant so much. They had been given a second chance. In both cases they deserved it.

Chapter 18

The day dawned crisp and bright. It was a light frost. The hunters moon, was a sight to see the night before, rising over the distant hills in the east, a great orb of red fused with amber. Liz was hoping for a dry night, because tonight was the Musical Evening at Innes Hall. She was looking forward to it but nervous even so. She felt the community around her was more important to her than the charity that she had hosted in the summer. A number of the villagers were walking to the concert, and last night's starry sky, Liz hopefully thought was going to make that possible.

Chairs had come from the village hall, in case they ran out of seating room. Even now the music room was filling up. It looked promising but Liz did not relax until the concert started.

The Vicar took over as Master of Ceremonies and the evening began with the Infant school choir taking centre stage. They sang their little hearts out. Their doting mothers and fathers were so proud, even with some of the participants forgetting at one point, their words. Lucky for the village, the Vicar's brother played the guitar, playing one classical piece and a medley of pop music, which went down well. The audience, old and young appreciated his playing. The Vicar's wife accompanied him on the piano beautifully.

Harry, although not being able to join Liz for the event, had managed to ask two of the operatic singers from his town's society, his firm being a patron, to sing some of the well known songs out of Gilbert and Sullivan. They jumped at the invitation and were well received. The senior boys and girls and the infants came together near the end of the concert singing, 'The WraggleTaggle Gypsies oh!' The seniors had been in attendance ushering the people to their seats and now the senior girls were helping with the coffee and biscuits. All in all, the evening was a great success and the little ones went home clutching a bag of sweeties.

The helpers tidying up next morning were full of it. Jane from the office had come up to the Music room to lend a hand. She had ferried some of the infants up to Innes Hall in her car the night before. Whether she would have attended is a different matter but Liz found out that she was keen on one of the young teachers from the school. They were much in evidence last night and Liz just wondered how long it would be before they would hear wedding bells.

'Thank you for helping to clear away Jane.' Liz said gratefully.

'That's all right. I had to come to the Music room anyway to collect the music to take back to the school later. Did you enjoy the evening?' she enquired of Liz, and then hurriedly asked.' 'And the infants?'

'Yes of course. We would have missed a treat if they had not sung. The evening would have had something missing. Don't you agree, and the senior choirs were excellent, weren't they?'

They smiled at each other as they left the Music room, Liz making her way to the Library and Jane heading off to the Office.

With the musical evening past, Liz realised that Christmas was looming in front of her. Christmas cards appeared in the stationers in the town where she ordered paper bags and wrapping for the shop. When she was there she asked when Innes Hall Christmas cards would be ready. This was a yearly occurrence. Innes Hall had dealt with this particular firm since the 1930's and it was still in the family. A rare thing in these days with the smaller shops being ousted by the giant stores, where one could purchase anything from a loaf of bread to a bedroom suite. This was because Liz thought, the head of the shop at the present time, was a well known figure in the community. He had two sons, and already one of them had joined his father. No doubt the second son would follow suit.

On the way home, Liz had to slow down to let horses and hounds pass in front of her. There were at least twenty followers on foot and a medley of cars, vans and estate cars blocking the road, coming the opposite way. The hunt materialised from nowhere. She stopped the car and enjoyed seeing the colourful array of the huntsmen in their scarlet coats trot through a roadside gate and start cantering. The huntsman giving a blast on his horn gathered up lost hounds as he went. An onlooker was holding open the gate for the remainder of the riders to pass. Liz was caught up with the excitement. The horses ranged from hunters to the cob, to the ponies that do the rounds at a Gymkhana, to the Shetland ponies bringing up the rear. A myriad of colours flashed before them, from black to bay to silvery grey, intermingled with the hunting pink and the assortment of smart black and tweed of the riders hacking jackets. The steam rising from the horses as they passed, only made the chase more exhilarating. Immediately passing into the field, horse and rider plunged down to the beck at the bottom, which bordered a thick wood opposite. The huntsmen had already straddled the beck and the hounds had gone into the wood. The familiar sounds of the hounds giving mouth denoted they had raised a fox or if not they were on to the scent. The chase was truly on.

From her vantage point on the road the valley was wreathed in sunshine. Most of the horses and riders were stilled and waiting. Suddenly, looking up to the far hill and having given the dogs the slip, or at least the spectators thought at that moment it had, the wily fox shot out of the wood at the other side and bolted up the hill. The huntsman gave the familiar blasts on the horn and the horses and riders dived through the thick undergrowth in the wood and out the other side. The fox was then, exposed with no shelter until it gained a wall parallel to the followers eagerly viewing the spectacle through their binoculars. Liz's heart quickened and her senses heightened. Although she loved the sport, she always liked the fox to give the hounds the slip. This always happened, because of the hunting laws, the huntsman calling off the hounds, allowing the escape.

At last after a considerable time the followers started up their engines and one by one they slowly moved off. Liz reluctantly started her engine going the opposite way, leaving the scene of horses and riders and the baying of the hounds echoing across the valley. It gave Liz a feeling of contentment, of wellbeing; to be here and now in the environment she had grown to love, to be one of the community. She had met her neighbours at the beginning. All were so welcoming. Liz had been roped in to village life as much as possible but being at Innes Hall, it was not too easy to down tools and be on this and that committee. Since John and she had parted company, Liz had thrown herself into the work in and around Innes Hall and with help from the staff, she was more than grateful that her position was safe.

The thought of Harry entered her head. These days though, she had to admit Harry was never really out of her head for long. For a moment she hugged herself. It was Harry that she had to thank for still being there. He could have easily terminated her contract saying it was for a married couple.

Then it would have been the end of it. A cold chill went through her. It would have been a dreadful situation to be in, but the secure knowledge that she was safe at Innes Hall meant everything to her. Liz had had to find her own feet, but in the past two years she had learnt so much. Nothing stopped her from tackling an issue that cropped up. Of course she had been bruised but she had come out the other side with new vigour. 'I wonder what brought this on' she thought, but she knew instinctively that she was the happiest in years. Liz stopped the car in front of the stout door and gathering up her shopping ran up the steps.

The nearer it got to Christmas the busier it became. Workmen were to be found inspecting the Hall's roof. John was in evidence with the men. They had access by the back stairs leading to a small door at the end of a short passage. This led to a permanent ladder out on to the roof. Liz had been on the roof soon after John and she had arrived. She had gone up to see the views the gardener had been telling her about. If she had known Edward and Denise then, she would have spotted where the stables were and pin pointed Innes Hall when Edward had driven them adjacent to the gallops on to the broad plateau. It was breathtaking looking down and across the rolling acres. Looking at the views at a different angle up on the roof, it had the same appeal. The immensity of it all was hard to take in at one go.

The day came when Edward and Denise went up to the Borders. Two days before Liz had them to supper and Harry had joined them. They were eager to get going and hand over the ropes to the new owner. Denise was hoping against hope that all the stable lads not going to Scotland would be mopped up by the new owner. It was a wrench for Edward and Denise to leave this lovely part of the country. They had made friends in the horse world, even Denise was fully committed where the administration was concerned, but she had a host of friends other than the racing fraternity. She was bound to feel sad at leaving, but as she said as she hugged Liz and said good-bye,

'It's a challenge we cannot miss.'

indication, no signpost directing visitors to its door, only in big bold black letters carved into the left of the entrance were the words, "The Hideaway." The façade of the hotel belied its name.

'How intriguing! It is a lovely name but I conjure up a low tiny place.' Liz had said, looking at Harry.

'Yes I would have thought that but I believe it is the rhododendrons that are grouped around the hotel. They are massive as you can see.'

Liz had soaked up the atmosphere. She had eaten luscious meats and savouries and sipped rich wines.

'What a beautiful place!' Liz had said, with eyes sparkling.

The sparkle though was natural under the circumstances with the man she loved, but a little must be awarded to the wonderful wines.

The bombshell had come at the end of the evening. Harry had driven up the drive to Innes Hall and switched off the engine.

'Liz' he had said 'There is something I must tell you and I would give anything not to have to. I am so sorry but,' he had paused anxiously searching her face that was catching the beam of light from above the door.

'Your job is no more.'

The words had sunk in only too well as Harry had spoken slowly and with deliberation. He had practically spelt it out. Liz had gasped, and her hands had grasped the dashboard. She had had the feeling of being tossed into nothingness, having lost all control. She had grappled with the feeling until the strangeness left her. She had managed to raise her eyes to Harry.

'You cannot mean it Harry?' She had questioned him futilely.

Harry had looked at her and said nothing. Liz had grabbed the car door handle and pushed it open.

'You said my job was safe.' she had stammered.

By now Liz was mechanically going through the motions. She had stumbled up the shallow steps and into the house slamming the door behind her shutting out Harry.

'Liz, Liz, I had to tell you, let me explain.'

It was useless staying on the doorstep any longer. Harry knew when to give up, and he had gone down the steps and driven off. Liz had not been able to control her sobbing. How could he let her think after the divorce even, that her life at Innes Hall was safe, so much for that she had thought. At that precise moment, Liz had hated Harry with such intensity. It was hard to believe but Liz had fallen asleep, exhausted, and had given herself up to oblivion.

As Harry had driven back to town he had been aware of the small square box holding the engagement ring in his trouser pocket. He had put it back in the drawer when he got back to the flat. Only hours before he had picked it up concealing it under papers out of the self- same drawer.

* * * * *

Liz woke to a loud knocking on the big front door. She put on her dressing gown while seeking her slippers with her feet. Her hair was dishevelled and her face was blotchy.

Opening the bolts on the heavy door Liz was overpowered and enveloped by Harry's strong arms. She gasped and cried out as his face swam before her eyes, fresh tears spilling down her cheeks. He just held her until the tears subsided.

Tossing and turning in her fitful sleep her thoughts had come to the conclusion that Harry would think the worst of her and even wonder at her fickleness. He might think twice of his future with her.

At last they drew apart. Liz backed into the entrance and turning her Harry put his arm round her shoulder and they started to walk over the marble hall. If anyone had seen them walking to the foot of the grand stairs, it was a rather unusual sight.

It was Harry who put the kettle on to boil and made the tea. Liz had splashed her face with cold water and emerged out of the bedroom looking more like her self.

'Come here,' and he caught hold of her left hand and slipped the engagement ring on her third finger.

'This, should have been already on your finger last night but everything went horribly wrong didn't it?'

Liz looked at the exquisite ring circling her finger, then looked up at Harry, then at the sparkling cluster of diamonds.

'Oh Harry!' Liz said. All worries were pushed aside and were forgotten as she went into his beckoning arms.

It was much later when Harry told her that he was leaving too and joining his family's firm in Edinburgh. Liz was speechless.

'You are leaving here and going up to Edinburgh,' she paused. 'Really!' She for a moment was flabbergasted.

'Yes, really! I wanted to tell you sooner, they have been expanding up there and they need me to fill a slot. I hope you don't mind being uprooted?' he asked.

Liz gave him her answer by going into his arms.

'I don't mind where I go as long as I'm with you.'

Chapter 20

It was common knowledge that they were engaged. One or two of the helpers in the house had an idea what was going on, even when Liz was missing for a full day when she was seen that morning, rushing out and going off in Harry's car, and ending up in Blackpool. All were over the moon. The main gardener said,.

'It's the best news I've heard for a long time.'

It was an extraordinary time for them both. If it were possible their love grew more between them. With ironing out the misunderstandings that Liz thought marred her happiness, being a little insecure at first perhaps, she could move forward now and never look back.

Harry and Liz could not make plans for themselves until Harry had told the staff what had occurred between the cousins. From his rooms, letters had been sent to all the farmers and all who were connected with the estate. All who could manage it were to come to Innes Hall, and those who had other commitments, letters would be sent to them on the day of the meeting. The timing was an important factor, not only to the cousins, but the tenants who occupied the farms and to the people occupying most of the houses in and around Innes Hall. True some would buy their houses others would have difficulties buying their farms at such short notice. Money was hard to find when all their capital was ploughed back into the farm.

So it was with trepidation and more than a little interest that they came together in the Great Hall. They had no idea what they had been called for. All this was supposition, but one man did say in passing, "I hope they are not wasting my time." Little did he know the colossal news, and the knock on effect it would cause in the close-knit community.

Harry started to speak. He gave a brief outline of every aspect of the sales that had to take place. Innes Hall and the park immediately surrounding it, all the beautiful furniture and effects and furthermore, most of the village as it belonged to Innes Hall and finally the school and farms which ran to thousands of acres were to be dispersed. One could hear a pin drop. Utter silence. Everyone was stunned and shocked. Then they all started to speak at once, not really making themselves heard because of their raised voices. Harry held up his hand.

'I think we all need a break. Coffee is laid on. Then I will try and answer your questions,' he said.

After coffee, which had been taken hurriedly, they quickly went to their seats, anxious to find out more. It was only dawning on them now what Harry had said. Their livelihoods were at stake. And what that meant to every individual in the hall was becoming apparent. A number of the tenants were hit badly. Others were knocked speechless. Generations of families would be broken up and nothing could be done about it. Not everyone had taken his seat until Harry was bombarded with questions.

'Why haven't we been told before now? Surely you must have known before this late stage?'

The man who was speaking was the man who minutes before had said 'I hope they are not wasting my time.' He was furious. He was big and stocky and he had a florid complexion. He was more florid now as he said his piece and then sat down.

Most of them in the body of the Hall had read scantily the documents. They were on the chairs when they grabbed their coffee. Others had refused coffee and had found out exactly where they stood, muttering to themselves, where on earth could they muster up the money. 'It would be nigh hand impossible' said a group huddled together. They could see nothing but to sell up. It would be impossible to find a farm in a matter of months before Candlemas. Of course they would try and buy their farms as they were sitting tenants but there were no guarantees they would be the final bidder and it would be knocked down to them.

A timid lady in the front row of seats spoke up saying.

'What has to become of the older people in the village? I for one cannot see my way to buy my cottage. If Lady Innes had been alive, this would not have happened, mark my words.' She collapsed into her chair after her outburst. It took some doing but she did want to make her point. The whole assembly agreed with her. It was hard for Harry to appease her, let alone the farmers. The gardeners and estate workers, all were affected. The workers on the estate asked would it be likely that they would be kept on. Harry had no concrete answer to that question. It was a possibility but their guess was as good as the next man when it came to that. There were no guarantees at the moment. Innes Hall was to be put up for sale, lock stock and barrel.

The nephew, had instructed his legal affairs officer, as soon as he had heard from Harry, to advertise the Innes Estate in the Big Apple. This sent a buzz through the great hall.

'Well if that is the case, we can say good-bye to all our farms if a "yanki" gets hold of them. He will rip out our dykes and hedges.' said a perturbed farmer. 'We've seen some of that already.'

'Oh, I don't know,' said another, 'he might just buy the whole estate and live in Innes Hall, and carry on as if nothing has happened.'

A joker amongst them said.

'We will look a fine sight rounding up the cattle on horseback. We are a motley crowd at the best of times.' He could not contain himself at the thought and burst out laughing.

The light relief was appreciated but the anxious, troubled looks were soon back on their faces.

Liz had been sitting at the back with the office staff and the ladies who managed the house and bringing up the rear the two ladies who manned the shop. It had flitted through her mind, John would have told the redhead about the engagement. She, up until now, would be on a high thinking Liz would be marrying soon and moving out, enabling her the right to move into the flat, although John was a little unsure of this fact. When she heard what had transpired when John arrived home that night, it would be undoubtedly a shock to her. They would talk well into the night. Not only John and the redhead would talk some more, but more to the point the farmers that could not see their way to buy their farms. It was more than one or two of the farmers who had racked their brains and voiced it at the meeting. It would be difficult at this time approaching their bank managers and being told of the climatic conditions, the borrowing rate they knew already. Could they see their way to cope with this tremendous weight on their shoulders? They were going to see him, even so. He was a good ally whatever they said about him. He might put something in front of them, new legislation maybe, doubtful, but worth picking his brains.

As the meeting finished and the groups finally dispersed, Harry gathered up his papers and went towards the office. He had brought with him a number of documents already sealed in their A4 envelopes. These were to be sent to the tenants who were absent. He was taking these to the office where they would be sent off by the afternoon post.

'It is a bit hard to take in, isn't it!' said Harry as he took his leave of them in the office and went back to the great hall where Liz and her helpers were stacking chairs.

'It has been quite a morning.' Harry addressed this to the helpers and to a few stragglers as they were going out. They nodded as they went.

A gloom settled on the whole estate. One could almost feel the atmosphere. When Liz waved Harry away, and turned and started up the grand staircase, the eyes in the portraits looked down at her. They lacked the lustre that she always thought they had. Now they were dark and sombre. Not even the young portrait of Lady Innes. She even had a scowl spreading over her face. Liz shivered. Surely there will be a light at the end of the tunnel for most of them! She cast her mind back only an hour when one of the older members of the village, voiced her concerns about her cottage. 'What would she do?' The lady had asked.

No one felt like doing any work in the afternoon. Liz didn't blame them and soon they folded up and went home. She had toyed with the idea of telephoning Denise when she got up in to the flat but decided against it. Things had snowballed and she had never told Edward and Denise of her engagement. Somehow she could not bring herself to impart the good news to them. Not yet anyway, not to day when she was thinking of the changes that would inevitably take place for everyone that had a connection with Innes Hall. Liz had a life with Harry to look forward to but some who had gathered this morning in Innes Hall, their outlook was decidedly bleak.

The days and weeks ahead were going to be tough for all concerned. To be truthful how could anyone think of anything else but the looming of the various sales that were to take place. It was the end of the next month and already it was going into the local papers and beyond. The local people were up in arms, they couldn't possibly get anything sorted out in that short time. That fact fell on deaf ears.

The viewing of the estate prior to the sale of the lots itemised in the catalogue was at 10am & 2pm Monday to Saturday, commencing the following Wednesday. By the following Wednesday a trickle of would be buyers were shown to the office door. It was hard to make out whether some of them were 'would be buyers' or not, or just here for the ride. By Saturday Harry had to draft in a colleague from his office, apart from two estate workers who were on the job to help.

All this time Innes Hall, the immediate grounds and the shop were being kept open and were being enjoyed by the visiting public. Surprisingly the takings had taken a jump. In all the departments the tills were full at the end of the day. Liz was in the office when the week's takings had just been totted up. Her eyes boggled at the amount. Some of the takings must be from the prospective buyers. She could only think that. It could only be said that the staff at Innes Hall were more aware of the difference between the regular public and the ones coming to Innes Hall for viewing purposes. More often than not they were asked for directions to the office if the stranger had taken the wrong turning in the house or in the precincts. The ladies in the sewing room didn't see much going on, closeted away in the confines of their cosy room. But on this Friday they got the shock of their lives, when a blustering big man, cigar in his mouth wearing a ten gallon hat burst into the tiny room. They both jumped at his quick entrance, their hands flying to their faces muffling a scream.

'Oh my good ladies,' he said in his American drawl, 'I am totally lost. I am looking for the office!' He was flustered at stumbling in on them.

After a moment, one of the ladies got to her feet slowly.

'Yes you did give us a fright.' She gave a nervous laugh looking at him. Apart from his stetson he was not as tall as first thought but his shoulders were broad. His body was long but he fell off at his short legs, but a handsome man at that the ladies observed.

'Come on I shall take you where you want to be.'

It seemed to all of them, when the Hall was closing down for the night and the public and the continual stream of people to the office had ceased, a stillness shrouded the whole building. Even 'it' knew there was to be a change. Briefly the feeling hung like a cloud and to the heightened senses it rubbed off on one and another. Unease crept in.

These days the ladies in the house were exhausted at the thoughts of splitting up the household effects. It would be sacrilege if that happened. They could not imagine any of the beautiful pieces leaving Innes Hall for good. When a piece of the finest of furniture or picture went out of the house, leaving a gap or a space on a certain wall, it was noticed straight away. These were always returned in due course after being lent to an exhibition, and as far as they knew none of the cousins had come to sort out or procure an item before the sale.

Liz saw Harry in the distance most days, either showing interested clients Home Farm or in the mornings in the office. After that it really depended on the viewers. The last fortnight he was further a field showing the other farms on the estate. In the village the properties were mainly owned by Innes Hall. This caused upset, when interest was shown by people from villages near by. This did not go down well when it involved some of the estate workers' cottages. It wasn't going to be easy showing a cottage that was home to them all their lives and in a few weeks trying to hold on to it on the sale day. It was worse still if they knew the interested party. The farmers and the estate workers would be sitting tenants but for how long. It would not be any length of time before their rents were renewed. They would have to leave because of the rents maybe. They wouldn't be able to see their way to come up with the extra that the Landlord wanted. Like Liz, they could not wait for the sale to be over and then at least they would know where they stood. Some were saying nothing, others were pushing the sale day to the back of their minds. Uprooting was alien to them. Liz felt for all of them. Her thoughts turned to Harry, she could have been in the same predicament if he had not come along. Thinking of him at that moment, urged her to run up stairs and sit down at the table and write to Edward and Denise.

*****

Dear Edward and Denise

Forgive me for being out of touch. I hope you are getting to know your way around the border country and getting to know your neighbours.

Now I can't keep my news from you any longer. Ecstatic is the word, I use in this case. I am so happy. Words are inadequate. One can't imagine just how happy I am now I am engaged to Harry but I am not dwelling on my happiness now, it is the second news that is earth shattering. Innes Hall is up for sale, lock stock and barrel. It may have filtered through to you already. The sale is imminent, the end of next month and we are going about our work half-hearted and despondent.

I have loads to tell, especially you Denise, 'girl talk', but we are hardly over the awful bombshell delivered us and the sale is getting nearer and nearer. If I hadn't met Harry I really think I would have run away. This is how desperate people are down here at Innes Hall.

Next time I shall telephone but I must stop. I feel I should be getting on with something, but what? It is too late.

Regards to you both, you lucky people and say, 'Hello' to the rolling hills for me.

Liz.

Helen Wood

****

'I wonder why the nephew is selling Innes Hall?' Liz thought so many times about this fact. Rumours were always flying around when a place like Innes Hall was discussed. She had asked Harry at the beginning and the only thing that was plausible to him was that the cousin in America decided to stay in America. This had caused a rift between the cousins. They said he should come home and take up where Lady Innes had left off. The result was they were not going to be penniless. They all had a stake in Innes Hall and whatever the Innes Hall Estate made, it would be divided equally between them. At first this wasn't the case but with pressure from cousins here and the wealth and livelihood that could not be found in England, plus keeping up the fabric of Innes Hall and its estate, he decided to sell and let them all have a share. It was the fairest way.

Chapter 21

The two sewing ladies, like every employee on the estate hurried to the sale in the marquee a little away from Innes Hall but this side of the river. Cars and Range rovers were pulled up on the road as far as one could see with the naked eye. The occupants were wending their way towards the marquee ready for the sale of Innes Hall. Mixed emotions were near the surface of all of them that were connected to Innes Hall. This was a day the whole community would remember all their lives.

The two sewing ladies took their seats and waited for the commencement of the sale.

'I wonder if our American will be here. I can't see him, can you?' said one of them.

'If he is, I wonder if he will think of us and keep us on?' said the other.

All the estate workers that could be at the sale were in full force bar the skeleton staff manning the house but more so the wealth of strangers was evident filling up the rows of seats.

The sale commenced at 11am. The cottages in the village and the village Post Office were first to be auctioned then the seven farms ending up with Innes Hall and the parkland. It was brisk bidding for all the various Lots and the farms sold well. Even with money being tight, there was wealth in and around the country. It was clear to see even here.

There was a break in the proceedings while the Auctioneer and his clerk totted up the Lots. As this was being done, the groups of tenants asked if anyone had kept track on the different amounts. One or two had but they were going to wait until the final result. Half of the farmers were not looking too worried at this juncture the others were resigned. They were hoping they would keep hold of their farms although some farmers had to go above the initial limit in some cases to secure them. It all depended what the estate as a whole would realise before anyone dared say with conviction a part of Innes Hall was knocked down to a member of the community waiting here in the tent. A feeling of unease swept through the rows of seats as the clock ticked away the time.

At last the auctioneer got to his feet. This time no one was keen to start the bidding.

'Would anyone like to give me an offer?' The auctioneer surveyed his audience so did his clerk.

Two rows down from the front, a dapper looking man was sitting in the aisle. When there was no interest, the man on the aisle listened to the auctioneer as he read out a statement. This statement had been handed to the clerk. It had come from the dapper looking man before the sale commenced and it materialised that he was the agent for a client. It transpired that the said client's offer had bought the Innes Hall estate. This stunned the people for a moment. It left them out on a limb, with no concrete answers given to them on the day. The employees who worked on the estate were hoping that the estate would carry on, as before, but there was always this niggling doubt while they waited to hear from the new owner in person.

The crowd dispersed slowly. It was noted about five or six strangers waited their turn to speak to the auctioneer and the clerk. This again caused raised eyebrows in the Innes community. What if one of them was a successful builder? If so he would try and buy a chunk of land from the new owner maybe and build row upon row of houses. The mind boggled at the thought. It would be best not to think a long those lines. It would be too painful for the older generation in the community to see that happen. The turf bit by bit eaten away as the buildings encroached. It was unthinkable. The heart of Innes Hall would slowly die.

The two sewing ladies let themselves into their domain. Like everyone else in the house, they felt deflated and exhausted. That was natural enough because before the event, they had had time to digest the enormity of the sale that was to take place. To come away with nothing really completed was to them baffling and another gruelling wait to find out their fate. Harry had gone back to town.

The nephew was to be informed of the outcome of the sale as soon as possible and this had fallen to Harry. He had told Liz that it was an American who had bought Innes Estates. Before Harry had left the marquee he had spoken to the auctioneer, and the agent. It turned out to be the same American who had burst in on the sewing ladies having lost his way. Liz had heard about the intruder bungling in on the sewing ladies when it had happened, right at the start of the viewing. Pleased to hear this from Liz they were a little elated. They had even talked to the new owner. None of the others had spoken to him to their knowledge and the ladies for a moment, thought back to the flustered state of the American that day, not to mention the fright they had got when he first appeared. But the fact remained it was too soon to speculate if their cottages and jobs were safe.

For the next fortnight the estate settled down. The community in and around Innes Hall had to get on with the day to day running. It had been a fraught time immediately after the sale, but it was business as usual. The ladies in the house asked Liz if she knew anything. She did not know anything either. Harry was waiting still for news from America. It came in the form of an American getting out of a silver sleek looking car, -with no exaggeration it was a mile long and stretched practically the full length of Innes Hall-, the same American with whom the sewing ladies were already acquainted. A rustle went through the big house. One of the ladies who was in the entrance moved away and quickly made her escape alerting who ever she saw in her path of the visitor. With him was Harry, and following up the rear was a young man who presumably was the son. Harry had telephoned Liz the night before of their arrival. She met them on the broad landing, leading to the flat. Introductions were made. John Brandt and his son, Wayne Brandt. The son, eager to see as much as possible especially the farms, went off with Harry to visit them, starting with Home farm. It turned out that the son had been in England studying land management at Cirencester.

After Harry and Wayne Brandt had gone, John Brandt, gladly took the offer of being shown around the house again. When he had been here before it had been a flying visit. This time Liz took him from room to room slowly. He had time to take in the beauty, the ornamentation and the immenseness of the house. He took more time in the old kitchens, glancing at the old range and then at the massive kitchen table. He showed his appreciation to Liz as they went, admiring the treasures that Innes Hall possessed and the views one could see from the windows. Liz did mention the view on the roof. That would be viewed when the American family were ensconced and had taken up residence.

John Brandt took his leave of Liz after she had shown him the house. He wanted to explore the gardens and the green houses. He had met the main gardener on his first visit and he made his way in that direction. Harry and Wayne Brandt did not appear until well into late afternoon. They had met John Brandt on the driveway and Harry parted company with them, arranging to meet them the following day at Innes Hall.

Harry went to the flat and found Liz cooking on the stove.

'I don't know who will be the more tired. I think though it will be neck and neck. I know the lie of the land but we have covered miles on foot. Wayne Brandt is terribly keen and I liked to see that in him. How did you get on with senior?'

'Oh grand.' said Liz. 'He was easy to get on with, and interested in the tour of the house. He had a good walk around the place the first time, but he did say, I had shown him much more which he had completely missed, for instance, the parlour through the door in the drawing room.'

Harry looked at her for a long moment, her face a little flushed from her labours at the stove.

'Come here.' he said and hugged her round her waist and kissed the back of her head.

'Don't!' Liz laughingly said and prised herself out of his grasp.

'I have made you bacon and eggs. You will be famished.'

As he finished the welcome meal he pushed his chair back and stretched his legs. He looked at his watch and said,

'I shall have to go Liz, but we will have to think of moving. Wont we? Why I am telling and asking you, is that the Brandts are coming to-morrow to set the wheels in motion and sign the final papers. After that there is nothing to stop them taking up residence here at Innes Hall. It will take some time for them to get here, but time will fly.'

Liz knew that this was going to happen but she had a pang or two.

'It will be strange when I leave the place for good and saying good-bye to all the friends I have made. Going out of the main gates for the last time will be awful too.'

'You'll get over it, and remember I shall be with you.'

'I know Harry, I know.' She swiftly came round the end of the table and urgently kissed him.

'How lucky I am, how lucky!' and her arms tightened round his neck'

'I am the lucky one darling Liz. You will never know how lucky.' As his mouth found hers, a tear escaped down Liz's cheek.'

The next day was busy. The fact that there was an unexpected deluge and the electricity failed only added to the situation. The thunder rolled and rattled around the heavens never giving up. It seemed the wrath of God was being aimed at Innes Hall. Visitors who were caught in the grounds and in transit to the shop and green houses ran for shelter. Visitors near the house scuttled up the main entrance. If it were possible, the thunder was loudest there, echoing along the corridors bouncing off one wall and then off the other. It came to the point that all who could amongst the helpers, were given giant candles to distribute into holders or go ahead of the paying guests to enable them to see their way on the tour of the house. It gave a new dimension as the candles held high, moved along. The candles as they flitted past the paintings brought out the colours of reds blues and sombre blacks, only to be followed by a gold shimmering light. For a split second it was there, then it disappeared. It left the onlooker doubting for a moment, whether one saw the shimmering light or was it a trick of the candles or the lightning. Milling and wandering around the house were the new owners. It was good for them to see how the day to day business of running Innes Hall was carried out. The son had an idea with being in England for some time but it was quite new to the father. He had never seen at close quarters this type of occupation. True he had heard of it but now seeing all these people eager to see everything and to take away the memory of the Hall and its contents, the idea of running Innes Hall in the same way took root. It would be sacrilege to do away with this facility said the son.

Very rarely had visitors been plunged into darkness. They would go away and could tell of their experience, not an ordeal but an exciting and to some, a magical one. They wouldn't even forget the old kitchens with their shadows and the candlelight playing on the glinting steel and copper utensils and the old kitchen range.

Normality came after four o'clock. The electricity was restored and the candles were extinguished, leaving a tallow smell for a while. The sun came out and miraculously dried the sodden surroundings with a piercing heat. By the time Innes Hall closed its doors to the visitors, it was hardly possible to cast one's mind back and believe that the dreadful storm had ever occurred. The sun was still high in the sky, not quite slipping in to the west, and the honeybees humming, gathering their last quota for the night. With Harry gone to town early, the Americans and the visitors had got into their cars and moved off. The one coach party from France that was

touring England climbed on the bus and the driver started up its engine and nosed it down the drive. Liz thankfully shut her flat door on the world. She slumped on the sofa and closed her eyes for ten minutes. It had been quite a day!

Liz was thumbing through the mail a week later and one letter was addressed to her. It was from Mr Frazer. He had been following the reports in the local papers of Innes Hall. It had been featured in the National newspapers where one of them had an article about the new owner. It went on to say the Hall had wonderful treasures and they had remained with the new owner. Straight away Liz lifted the telephone and rang him.

'My time here is running out, and the new owners want to take up residence, as soon as possible.' said Liz.

He was genuinely sorry to hear this from Liz.

'How is that young man of yours? What does he think? Of course he would be in close contact with the nephew until the sale went through.

'Yes he has.' said Liz. 'But Harry has been with the son Wayne Brandt these last few days, going to all the farms. As for me, well.' she hesitated a smile broadening over her face, as she said to Mr Frazer down the telephone, 'We are.' and before she could say anymore she heard him say.

'You don't mean to tell me, you are tying the knot?'

Liz could not suppress the warm feeling when Harry was mentioned.

'Yes we are. I have been to my favourite place a lot of times hoping to find you there to tell you our news but you were never there. I am so happy Mr Frazer.'

'I can tell that now from your voice. Tell him from me, what a lucky fellow he is.'

Liz placed the receiver on the rest and sat down on the sofa. Mr Frazer had listened to her highs and lows and she valued his friendship. He had taken over where John's father had left off she realised. Briefly she thought of John's father and hoped he was all right and well.

Chapter 22

Liz looked around the flat for the last time and then closed the door. She ran down the grand staircase across the marble hall and out of the front door. Harry was waiting for her with the car door open. Their destination that night was to break the journey and stay with Edward and Denise. The night before Harry and Liz had said their good byes at a small get together in the Music room. They had been presented with a picture of Innes Hall and what Liz marvelled about was the fact that most of the immediate helpers plus the gardeners were taken in front of Innes Hall in the photograph. That in itself was a mystery because Liz, to her knowledge, never saw a photographer taking the photograph.

The Brandts were already in England staying not too far from Innes Hall. Mrs Brandt had been thrilled, proud, and amazed all at once.

'How magnificent.' she drawled in her deep American accent.

Only a few personal items of furniture were coming over the water, as more would be superfluous. The Brandts intended to live most of the year at Innes Hall but occasionally fly back to their old home in America and visit friends and relatives.

Harry and Liz had spent a day with Mr Fraser, having driven over to where he lived. It had taken them a good part of the day, getting there and back, but it was worth it. Mr Fraser had shown them around the village and the church, ending up down by the river. They had walked a little way when the path narrowed leading to steps. There were six in all. Bending their heads they had gone through an aperture into a cave. At first they were in darkness until their eyes got accustomed to the shadows. On the facing wall one could see faint drawings, but they were so faded that it was impossible to really see what they were. It was said a monk visited the cave when he was in the area but all sorts of stories were spun about it.

Before Harry and Liz said good-bye, they had asked Mr Fraser if he could make it to Edinburgh for their celebrations. He said he would be delighted. He had said, just tell me the day and I shall be up to see you tie the knot.

Liz had written a long, long letter, cramming all the news past and present, to Nigel and his aunt, ending up with their imminent departure to Edinburgh. No sooner had the letter gone than a reply had arrived.

'Thrilled for you both. Keep in touch will you? I know it is a long way, but distance is no object these days. My door is always open.'

Liz had given Harry the letter to read.

'Who knows, we might well do that, land on their doorstep? I know you would like that,' he said.

Soon the built up areas were receding fast as the car gathered speed. It was a glorious day to be starting off on another chapter of their lives. Liz looked at Harry and wondered if he had thought that too.

'What is it?' he asked.

'Well it struck me that we are starting out together, really together, you and I, a new chapter.' She stopped there and waited for him to speak.

Harry glanced over at her and he gave her a dazzling smile.

'Yes, I have you all to myself.'

They made good time to Carlisle. The city was bustling. They had seen cattle wagons making their way to the Auction Market and at the Town Hall stalls were set up and shoppers were milling around. In one place it was so crowded one could only see the tops of the stalls. Towering above this scene were the mighty walls of the castle and the cathedral, their eyes fixed never straying from the activities of the city. It was nearing lunchtime and Harry and Liz hurried to a restaurant opposite the Cathedral, hoping they would get a table. They were lucky but other people were streaming in behind them. They had a leisurely meal, Liz having salmon on a bed of fresh salad and Harry enjoying the steak.

'That was good,' Harry declared. 'I must admit I was ready for it.'

After looking at what Carlisle could offer in the way of shops with the sun on their backs, they slowly retraced their steps taking in the Cathedral. They were lucky as they joined a party with a guide moving off a few yards from the entrance. It was learnt that Carlisle Cathedral was the second smallest. Only two bays survived of the original seven, they were told. Carlisle preserves one show piece, and that is, its east window. It is described as the finest in the kingdom. They were shown forty-six 15th century, well maintained stalls, with big and lively misericords, and looking upwards a wagon-roof attractively painted.

Harry and Liz came out of the cool Cathedral, the sun more powerful than when they went in. The weather forecast was good for several days it said that morning when Liz was having her cereal. For a moment she thought of Innes Hall then turned to Harry and said.

'I feel I have been away from Innes Hall longer than it actually is. Do you feel like that?'

Harry considered her question and then said.

'Well yes, and no, but I have got used to the idea because I have known longer about leaving the Practice and it is home to me where we are going.'

They had moved out of the grounds and were sitting on the wall surrounding the Cathedral. Liz for a moment thought of Harry's parents. She would be a Sassenach amongst them. For the first time nervous tension gripped her.

'Harry,' she blurted out. 'Your parents will like me?' She waited to hear confirmation trying to read his face, a warm pinkish glow slowly spreading across her face. Harry gripped her shoulders.

'Of course they will. They are longing to meet you and I am dying to show you off to my friends.'

They left Carlisle steeped in history and crossed Eden Bridge, and made their way out of the city. It wasn't long until they were met with "Welcome to Scotland."

'That was quick. I thought we had to go a few more miles.' said Harry.

Liz had got the map out of the pocket nearest her, and she was studying it, she nodded to him.

'I think I know where we are, we veer left before too long, and I have seen glimpses of the sea, the Solway Firth.' She paused and then looked at Harry. 'What a perfect day to be travelling with this breeze.'

After the heat of mid-day, it was lovely to feel it on their faces through the half open car window.

With the road map on her knee Liz had calculated wrongly. It was at least thirty miles further on when they found the proper turn off on the left.

Harry had dropped to thirty miles an hour as the road curved this way and that, and it was considerably narrower. The sound of the traffic that had been with them all the way, suddenly ceased. As they went deeper on the secondary road, Liz looked over her shoulder trying to see any of the traffic they had left behind. Instead she saw tall trees and hedges that they had passed, enveloping their car, shutting out all noise and visibility. She turned to face the front and only the bonnet of the car fleetingly caught the full glare of the sun. The road widened in parts and just as it was thought safe to put down one's foot, Harry was confronted with three bends and a signpost indicating a village three miles away. The road straightened and they passed a few straggling cottages.

'I am sure this is the village before we go over a bridge. Denise said the racing stables were after that and they are well posted,' said Liz, trying to see any building and even horses in the fields.

Passing through the village Harry gathered speed. The said bridge was ahead of them. Dipping down to it, the car went over it, and they found they had passed over a river. At the other side, plain to see was the sign to the racing stables. Turning right, they headed up a rickety track. On they went not gaining much speed until the road broadened and the surface was visibly smoother. It seemed that two farms, one on the left and another a little further on, had the same access as the one leading to their destination hopefully.

'We are coming closer I think,' Harry said. 'I've noticed buildings and some horses. Look through the hedgerow,' and he pointed to his side of the road.

'Well we must be surely there, nearly,' Liz said, excitement rising in her voice, as she looked at Harry.

He smiled at her, and knew instinctively what a visit to Edward and Denise meant to her. Although they had not been up in Scotland for long, Liz had missed the girly chats she and Denise had had in the past. Low buildings loomed in the dip of the road. Ahead of them large double white gates flanked the road. They went through the gates into the stable yard. Not a soul to be seen, but it was understandable as the work in the stables was finished for the day. Only one or two of the horses had come to the half opened doors to see who had arrived. They looked like inquisitive busy bodies. Their interest satisfied they turned back into their boxes. It prompted Liz to say to Harry.

'I wonder where Old Boy is? He must be somewhere.'

On the opposite side of the stable yard there was another white gate, and through that, they saw the house facing them. It was built of grey stone and it had three gables along the front. The front door was set a little way in, and a stout porch jutted out to shield it from the weather.

Edward and Denise must have been looking out for them at that moment, because as they drew up and Harry switched off the engine, they came out to greet them.

'Have you had a good journey?' they asked.

'A good one and the weather has been glorious.' said Harry shaking hands with Edward.

'So good to see you.' How are you both?' asked Liz, hugging Denise.

'Settling in remarkably well considering, but Denise has yet to walk the boundary. She has been busy doing something in the house which has taken up much of her time.'

'I'll show you Liz what I have been doing later but Edward and I were thrilled to hear your good news.'

They had all moved inside and Edward was pouring champagne into glasses to toast the happy pair. Edward and Denise could see how happy, Harry had made Liz. They ate and chatted well into the night. Harry told Edward about the farms that had gone under the hammer and Liz was able to tell Denise about the Hall being saved and not split up.

'I only hope the American keeps on all the staff. That is my only worry. I might have been one of them.' Liz paused a second and looked at Denise, 'I honestly don't know what I would have done.'

The next day Denise showed Liz what she had been doing to the house in the way of decorations. She had stripped the floorboards of their dark colours and given them a fresh coat of lighter stain.

'It made all the difference Liz. Much lighter too, with the white walls and paintwork. Did you notice we are in a hollow here and with an abundance of trees around us, I thought on winter days it would brighten up the house. Although saying that the brown paint that I scraped off, it did hide the dirt.'

'What a lot of work Denise! Did you get anyone to help?' asked Liz.

'I was so lucky. I was scraping away, it was this floor actually, when John, one of the stable lads came looking for Edward. He saw what I was doing and before I knew it, two of them helped me out in their spare time.'

'Denise! Wasn't that great of them.' Liz said.

'Really it was. I think if John had not seen me labouring away, I would still be doing it. They did work hard and this is the result. I am really pleased how things turned out.'

'You should be,' said Liz.

In the afternoon Edward suddenly said that it was a perfect day to walk the boundaries.

'A great opportunity to get Denise out of the house after doing the decorating and I think, Harry and Liz.' he paused and then continued, 'Although you have been used to rolling hills, we think you will like the surroundings here.'

They set off at the front of the house through the stables and skirted some outbuildings leading to the fields. Once there, they were in the open. For a while the ground was flat and then the vista changed visibly. The trees were falling away and there was a steep but short climb to the top of the field. Once gained the party could hear the murmurings and just see at that point the river in the bottoms of the undulating fields. The river, curving and twisting, splaying out in places, toyed with rocks and lesser big stones, relentlessly surmounting its labours.

'Over there.' said Edward lifting his hand to the left 'I think you can see a strip of water, that is the Solway.'

'Yes we can see it. It does not seem far away.' said Harry.

'No, but the river turns back on itself and we lose it. It comes into view at the other side of the buildings and meanders along under the road and eventually empties into the Solway.'

'Nearly everyday we take the horses down to the Solway for a good gallop. The seawater does their hooves the world of good and believe me, they love the splash as they enter the water.' added Denise.

At that moment Old Grey came into Liz's mind.

'Edward, where is Old Grey? I half expected to see him before now. Where is he hiding?'

'He is enjoying life looking after a number of brood mares. He is in his element. He is over in the back field behind the house.'

That evening Edward took Harry to a quiet hotel for an amiable drink and chat with his new found friends. Meanwhile Denise and Liz chatted happily about the wedding and before Harry and Liz left the next morning Denise and Edward were going to be most important guests at the wedding.

'And we mean that, don't we Liz?' Harry had said in parting.

'We do.' and she stressed the, we do, in her voice.

'I don't know how I would have managed at first Denise. It was a lucky day when we met in the Post Office, wasn't it?'

Liz hugged them both and then got into the car with Harry and drove away.

The weather was still holding dry. The whole of England and Scotland was bathed in warm sunny weather. Even when the weather forecast came on after the news on television, there was not a vestige of a cloud in the blue sky shown.

Liz had never been out of England for any length of time into Scotland. All was new to her. As they ate up the miles, the scenery was breath taking. Looking straight ahead, the road was blocked by the beginnings of a steep mountain range making them zigzag to the left and then to the right. All this time they were climbing steadily. At last the sheer rock face fell away and Harry stopped the car for Liz to admire the view. At one side of the road, it fell away into a deep ravine.

'This is the Devil's Beef Tub.' Harry said.

They got out of the car and went across the road to take a longer look at the expanse and the void of the gouged out crater. Liz was grateful for Harry's arm to hang on to as the drop made her dizzy. She strained her eyes and saw sheepfolds at intervals on the floor of the Devil's Beef Tub. How aptly named. Liz well imagined the awful rustling and the fighting between the different clans.

'Gosh Harry, what dreadful times they were. Fancy living in those days.'

'You mean the cattle raids between the different clans? They would have to be on their guard all the time, wouldn't they?' added Harry.

As they motored on further, high on a rise where the old road used to be, is erected a monument in memory of James McGeorge, Guard and John Goodfellow, Driver of the Dumfries to Edinburgh mail. They lost their lives in the snow after carrying the bags so far, in 1891. Harry pointed to the monument half way up the hill. Liz imagined the terrible turmoil and plight they would be in but ever hopeful they would get to their destination. It had not to be. Oh those poor men, what a tragedy she thought.

The road was deserted in places and roadside cottages were few and far between. Tracks leading off the road lead to crofts and one entrance with the name The Mains. Looking well into the distance following the winding road where one could, suddenly the farmstead was exposed lying on the hillside surrounded by a wilderness of heather and wet moss. As they ate up the miles Harry saw a garage and he pulled in for petrol. As he unwound the cap off the petrol tank the mechanics he saw were busy with umpteen cars but one of them came over to them. The accent was not totally alien to Liz as one of the estate workers had moved down from the far north and he had never lost his accent. Liz was sure this attendant had done the same to find work. Moving off on to the road again, the traffic was getting heavier and leaving the garage behind they soon came to a village. Looming ahead there was a crane and dumper machines. There were three big lorries ready to move off, loaded with rubble but still tons of rubble to cart away off the site. Obviously industry was about to set up business in the village.

'When we are married and settled in, we will come back to this area. You will like it. There are some rugged and beautiful places to see off this main road.'

Approaching Edinburgh to the left the Pentland hills rose gently behind a frieze of firs and pines and in front of that, one could see at intervals golfers on the golf course taking aim at the ball with their golf club or walking to the next flag in the distance. A peaceful scene it seemed but to the golfer, she or he would be always striving to lower their handicap no doubt. On the outskirts of Edinburgh at Fair Mile Head, Harry turned the car up a short drive and stopped at the front door of a house.

'We are here Liz. Come and meet them. It's a wonder they are not outside at the back of the house lapping up the glorious weather.'

Suddenly a dog gave mouth and it swiftly bounded around the corner of the house and jumped up at Harry.

'Down Jasper, down. You must not jump up at Liz like that. You will nearly knock her over.' He pushed him away gently and smiled at Liz.

****

Harry's parents were both tall and striking. They welcomed Liz with open arms. Harry's mother secretly had wished so long for this day. She had despaired of her son ever bringing a girl back to the house but she had worried unduly. Liz was all and more than she wished for as a daughter-in-law and what is more she saw how much Harry adored her.

The next few weeks Harry's mother took Liz out and about delighting in showing her off to her many friends. Meanwhile Harry was getting familiarised with his father's domain and meeting up with his colleagues old and new. His father's office was off Princes Street. Harry did notice his father had taken over another suite of rooms next door making it a bigger concern, hence the few fresh faces. As the weeks flew by, and they did in quick succession, Harry and Liz had been out and about visiting Harry's friends and he showed her his old haunts and his old school. One time they had been leaning over the ramparts of the castle, Liz marvelling at the views. How Edinburgh sprawled itself, its tendrils stretching to the north, the south, the east and the west. Arthur's Seat behind the castle guarding Edinburgh, the Pentland Hills, and the Firth of Forth, a silver strip meeting the sky in the distance. Looking down from their vantage point, the magnificent vibrant city was heaving with pedestrians thronging the pavements of the streets and spilling into the manicured gardens of Princes Street watching for the cuckoo to come out and cuckoo the hour on the flower clock.

One day Harry dropped her off in Princes Street. She had the day to herself and Harry was meeting her at four o'clock. The day stretched in front of her. She found herself climbing the steps and entering St Giles Cathedral. It was early in the day but tourists as well as the congregation who were making their way into the body of the cathedral to morning service, were studying their guide books. They were hoping to remember every detail even not in the guidebook but seeing it with their own eyes was a bonus to them. Liz joined them glorying in the fact that she was actually there in St Giles Cathedral soaking up the atmosphere within its mighty walls.

Liz walked along Princes Street after leaving the cathedral and then crossed over to the Tartan Shop. Harry's mother had pointed it out to her when they were hurrying to meet friends of hers last week. In front of the shop what intrigued her, was a board with all the names of the clans and their tartans starting with Adam. This was amazing to Liz and she spent time reading the tartans before moving on to a dress shop. Her intention as she set out this morning was to buy something special for her wedding. Her senses heightened as she took in the rows of light coats and dresses that were on display. Liz was waiting for the attendant to bring a selection but when she saw them the garments were too drab and really not what Liz had in mind. She plucked up courage.

'I really want something airy fairy.' She stopped and smiled.

'I am looking for something for my wedding. Not white but something special.' Liz ended.

'How wonderful.' The attendant said, leaving Liz and coming back with a number of lovely creations.

'I think these are more to your liking.' She said.

Liz tried three of them on and it was the third one that caught her breath. Her reflection looked back at her. The attendant was speechless for a moment then she said.

'I never thought how lovely you would look in that yellow.'

Liz looked at herself again and then said.

'I never knew either until now.'

Liz left the dress shop on a high. She could have hugged the assistant as she left her, she having joined in the search finding her the perfect white dainty shoes and accessories. Liz left her purchases in the assistant's care until nearer the day of her wedding. Tomorrow she and Harry were going house hunting. This sent a tingle up and down her spine even just thinking of it, having a house that belonged to them both, choosing it together, either big or small and then furnishing it bit by bit. The rent that came from the house each month would help a long way in acquiring furniture and the umpteen utensils that they would need. At Innes Hall Liz had left anything that had been hers, as the flat had been adequate, being furnished already and the house she now owned was let fully furnished. Harry's parents had shown them two properties that they had seen in the local paper.

Armed with the paper lying on the back seat they headed off to the Estate Agents. Harry and Liz were shown a number of houses, some big, others smaller. The photographs all were doing justice to them and they picked out three properties that were free to view.

The first one was a big substantial town house in a row. These were all maintained to a high standard. The reception rooms were light and airy and faced south. Some of the rooms were in need of decorating but that did not seem to matter to Liz. The only comment Liz had to say and it was a point to consider, it would take a lot of heating. The second house was similar but smaller, but the back of the property was cramped and only a small door for an entrance was found at the rear. It had two reception rooms but lacking a third room downstairs. Still it had all the amenities and at a pinch anyone could move in straight away.

In the afternoon Harry and Liz had to meet the agent back at the office. He had lined up for them a house on the outskirts of Edinburgh. He was taking them to see it. They were aware that it was a little dilapidated from the picture that they had seen at the office but the agent said it would be worth seeing. Hence the car turned off the main road coming to a stop after three miles. The house was seen through an overgrown garden. Stepping up on to the shallow front door step, the agent ushered them in to a wide lobby and half way along the stairs went up on the right. He tried the electric light and it immediately switched on. His partner had been showing interested clients around that morning so did not switch off the electrics at the main. It had been dark in the lobby until it was flooded with light. The three of them went from room to room, upstairs and down, the agent leading the way. In the kitchen and the back lobby dark green linoleum was on the floors. It had seen better days being frayed in places. It reminded Liz of the exact green covering her school floors in the form rooms. She mentioned this to Harry.

'Our school had this up and down stairs and I remember one of the maids once a week used to put some sort of polish on it and then buff it off.' Liz indicated by spreading and pointing her hand to the floor.

Along the wide lobby leading to the stairs, it was stained wooden boards. Each side of the steps of the stairs were also stained, only leaving the treads untreated where the stair carpet had been. It was a straight stairway and instead of a large staircase window, it was less than a normal sized window being obliterated by, when Harry went closer and peered through the panes, a big branch which was blocking out the day light.

'That must go. The first on the list of priorities Liz.' Harry laughed at Liz and she said smiling up at him.

'Are you warming to this property Harry?'

'Indeed I am, Liz.' Harry said in a playful manner.

'Well you will be in your element. There were dozens of trees outside with their branches ready for lopping as we walked up the path.' She ended. A giggle rising in her throat was hard to suppress.

The agent went ahead of them opening all doors to the left and the right of them. All rooms looked a decent size with tall ceilings upstairs and downstairs. The agent then said.

' The house has been empty for six months but it hasn't harmed in any way. There are no damp patches anywhere and the roof is sound. A desirable place anyone would say but come outside, I want to show you what it offers at the back of the house.'

Harry and Liz followed him through the kitchen and back premises and out at the back door. They both remarked as they went through the house, every door was solid and when shutting them they clicked tight. The back door when they came to open it had a mortise lock and two bolts top and bottom, the same Harry noticed when they came through the front door.

The weeds did not have any bother growing between the cracks of the flags. The agent and they were met further down the path with practically the beginnings of a hayfield. The garage and a garden shed were down at the bottom of the path and when they reached there, they saw a back entrance to the left for a car. The agent opened the garage doors to let them see inside and Harry and Liz were surprised, how big it was. It would easily house a car and have room enough for storage.

The evening was taken up with the three properties Harry and Liz had seen that day. Harry's parents were keen to hear how the viewing had gone.

'Well Liz liked the three of them. The two houses were bang in the centre of Edinburgh up side streets, so handy for work. Tree lined and not too noisy. The first one was bigger than the second one and needed a lick of paint and the second one we saw, we could have moved in straight away.'

Harry went out to the car and brought in the leaflets showing the picture and details of the three houses.

'And what did you think of them Liz?' asked Harry's father.

'I liked them all but we more than liked the third house when we finally saw it, didn't we, Harry? We would like you to go with us and give us your opinion before we go ahead.'

Liz caught hold of Harry's hand hardly daring to think of the possibilities of them not liking it. Father finding a major fault that they had missed the previous day would be awful and mother would agree with him although she would feel wretched for us. When they saw the property yesterday and moved about in the house she and Harry had felt the house was waiting for them to move in. At least they had made up their minds there and then individually and were dying to tell each other. It was soon after Harry had voiced it. They had travelled home making plans to sign on the dotted line after talking to the parents. Harry and Liz were anxious and excited all at the same time. They held each other tightly before Liz turned and went up stairs, the next day was crucial to them. The wedding day was getting nearer and it would be ideal after the celebrations to move to the house even if any decorating had to be done then.

The parents moved around the house inspecting all the nooks and crannies. Father and son at one time were outside viewing the drainpipes and the slates on the roof. Father could not see at a glance any real faults that would stop them to reconsider their choice. In the house, mother was saying to Liz, soon to be daughter – in - law.

'I am thrilled for you both, if you really like it and the price is right, grab it before someone else takes an interest.' She finished.

'I hope we can too. I hope father does not find fault with any of the exterior.' Liz said anxiously.

'You know Liz, when we were looking for a house we were just like you. I can remember traipsing round the country until we found one and fell in love with it. We relied on a friend to tell us if he would buy it if he were looking for a place. We were glad when he said to go ahead. It was further down the coast road and we lived there for five years until we moved to Edinburgh. We loved it there. Harry was born there and we regretted in a way moving to Edinburgh. It would have been a lovely place for him to grow up in.' ended Harry's mother.

Before getting in the car they looked back at the house through the jungle of trees. Harry and Liz had nothing detrimental to think about after hearing father and mother's verdicts.

'We will come on Sunday Liz and make a start on the grass. I think we will have to bring a rake but did you see the assortment of implements at the back of the garden shed? We will sort them out but I don't think they are much good else the people who lived here would have taken them with them.' said Harry.

Father intervened.

'Are you two not forgetting something? What about first of all, hurrying to the Estate Agent and putting an offer on the table? Didn't you say one of you, there was another party interested and they had seen the property in the morning? When it has been on the market for sometime the agent will be anxious to get it off their hands. It might be gone for all we know.'

'Oh no father, surely not but just in case, Liz and I will go to the agent's office straight away tomorrow.' said Harry, both he and Liz looking concerned with what father had just said.

With transactions taking longer, the other party had put in an offer there and then, the agent told them this when they arrived. This made them more anxious as the other party had given a firm offer when they had returned to the office.

'Are you prepared to up the price?' Said the agent.

'Yes certainly, we want it desperately.' They said, consternation on both their faces.

Nothing could be done that day. The lady of the house said that her husband was away and was expected back either Thursday or Friday. She could not give a concrete answer. Harry and Liz left the office hoping that the agent had good news after he had spoken to the husband at the end of the week. They just hoped their offer would be accepted, knocking out the other party.

Harry had been working alongside his father finding out the different firms and private clients who were placed with them. Leafing through the ledgers he saw beautiful copper plate writing denoting a different age and clients and firms bang up to date, their details and correspondence stored on computers and discs. He had done this familiarising since he and Liz had come up to Edinburgh. Being a solicitor he knew one day soon he would be seeing clients in this establishment, either old clients or new ones who had been recommended to the practice. It was in these rooms when the call came through from the Estate Agency. It had taken a full fortnight before the agency had got back to Harry.

'It is yours if you still want it. Sorry about the delay. The other client did want it but could not see his way to offer any more. He had reached his limit and he regretfully withdrew.' The agent ended.

No sooner the house was signed over to them Harry and Liz rushed to the house and threw open the widows. They swept and mopped dozens of times until it was fresh and clean and Harry's mother and Liz took a few pots and pans and a kettle to make tea. It was surprising how the different rooms were taking shape. A table and two chairs in the kitchen and odd easy chairs Harry had picked up at a saleroom at the end of the street. A bedroom suite and double bed had been delivered when they had both been hacking down the branches letting in the light. It was then they realised the wedding day was fast approaching. They intended moving in the day they came back from their honeymoon. Harry and Liz did a tour of the house before they finally locked the front door. Next time they would be returning and taking up residence. Liz could hardly wait to start the decorating although with the mopping and washing of windows and Harry lopping and pruning the branches in the garden, the whole property had an airy and looked after appearance.

****

The day before the wedding Harry was to drop Liz off at the hotel where she was staying the night. He was going for a drink with the boys. It was only now Harry turned to her, emotions running up and down his whole being.

'This time tomorrow, we will be nearly married darling Liz.' He caught her tightly to him.

Covering her upturned face with his kisses, he sought her lips with such force Liz drowned in that moment. She had never been transcended in this way, lifted up on to a higher plane. The new feeling was being transmitted through Harry to her clinging body. It touched emotions that fired her inside, reaching the depths of every avenue. Suddenly they drew apart visibly shaken. Their bodies experiencing the tug of each other, the frustrating feeling was evident in their faces.

Harry finally left Liz at the hotel, she rang the dress shop and soon her wedding finery was safely in the wardrobe. She sat down to wait for Mr Frazer, Edward and Denise. Liz hardly could believe that this morning Harry had imparted true love to her, releasing the final strands of reticence within her. Her love for him was complete. She started to count the hours before she saw him again.

Liz was attracted by the swish of the swing doors. She saw Mr Frazer first, followed by Edward and Denise. She jumped up and ran to them, a hint of tears misting her lovely eyes.

'I've missed you so much,' Liz said to Mr Frazer looking up at him and giving him a fond hug.

'It is lovely to see you all once again,' turning to Edward and Denise then. 'And I hope you are looking forward to tomorrow.' she ended.

'Of course we are.' they said in unison, and then Mr Frazer said,

'I am truly honoured to give such a sweet lovely girl away on her wedding day. I shall be so proud.'

Chapter 23

In the privacy of her hotel bedroom, Liz looked at the dress she was going to wear for her wedding hanging outside the wardrobe door. It was an empire line dress reaching to the ankles. The colour being the palest of yellow with a gold thread outlining a sequence of little embroidered flowers. The excitement bubbled up inside her. She caught her breath. 'Oh! I don't think I shall ever get to sleep tonight.' she said to herself. Liz thought about her old life at Innes Hall. It was receding rapidly into the background as her new life was emerging. Thinking of the staff at Innes Hall, without them, it could not have achieved any of its goals. Liz was sure the Americans would keep its standards and most important was the charity in the way of functions. Looking back Innes Hall was a thriving community not one that was declining. Liz hoped the worries of the staff had been unfounded and they were all pulling together once more. Briefly she thought of John and the red head. There was no malice, even if the red head had nearly driven her to distraction. Before she fell asleep she murmured to the still room. 'Good luck, Innes Hall.'

No sooner had she fallen asleep she was woken by voices outside the bedroom door. Liz looked at her watch and sprang out of bed. Quickly rinsing her face and combing her hair, she grabbed her bag and room key and hurried down stairs into the dining room for breakfast. She scanned the tables to see if Edward and Denise were at a table but there was no sign of them. Liz did not expect to see Mr Frazer either, until half an hour before her wedding when he would arrive and 'whisk her away' to the ceremony. They had laughed happily last night when Mr Fraser had said those words as they got into the lift and said good night.

Denise looked at her watch and hurried to Liz's room and knocked on the door. It was opened by a smiling bride- to-be, fully dressed. In her hair tiny yellow rose buds attached to a slide.

'Oh Liz!' Denise caught her breath. 'Liz you look stunning.'

Liz caught her hand and she gave her a quick hug.

'Look.' she said as she picked up an ivory prayer book from the dressing table, this was my mother's prayer book. My father gave it to her on their wedding day, and I am going to carry it on mine with this one yellow rose.'

'What a lovely thought and how appropriate.' said Denise. 'Now then, are you sure you will be alright until Mr Fraser comes for you?' she added. 'I should be downstairs in the foyer, Edward is waiting for me.'

At that, there was a knock on the door, and it was Mr Fraser.

'How did you know where I was?' Liz asked him.

'That was easy. I told the receptionist I had an important ceremony to attend giving a bride away. Then I met Edward and he told me which door to knock on.'

'You look gorgeous! I must fly.' Her eyes were a little more than bright as Denise went through the door and quickly got into the lift.

As they settled into the car for the short drive to the ceremony, Mr Fraser glanced at Liz sideways.

'I am the proudest man in Scotland I can tell you.' he said.

Liz leaned over and gave him a fleeting kiss on his cheek and said.

'I am the luckiest girl having you to give me away.'

As they entered, Harry and the best man Mac, his cousin, rose and moved out into the centre aisle, both looking dashing in the kilt and wearing their dress tartan. Turning towards Mr Fraser and Liz they waited until they came to stand beside them, Mr Fraser relinquishing his arm from Liz to stand next to Denise who was Liz's matron of honour.

The ceremony was brief and simple, not elaborate by any means. All who attended the service came away feeling they had witnessed a beautiful ceremony with Harry and Liz making their vows, and it was made possible to a greater extent by the minister, having got to know the circumstances and the breakdown of Liz's marriage before. Liz and Harry had gone to see him to ask if he thought they could be married in church.

It was the happiest of days. Toasts were raised to the Queen and then to the happy couple. Letters and messages had been handed in by a busy postman that morning, and were being read out by the best man. Amongst these, one was from Nigel and his Aunt, wishing them well and hoping to see them in the near future in Italy. Another one was from John's father. Liz wasn't too surprised hearing from him, although their acquaintance was cut short. Last and thrilled to hear from them all, everyone at Innes Hall and the surrounding district who had connections with it. It was truly a day Harry and Liz would remember forever. They were stepping out, starting a new chapter and a new life together.

The End.